All Time Summer

All Time Summer

ANNSHEE

PARTRIDGE
A Penguin Random House Company

Print information available on the last page.

To order additional copies of this book, contact
Toll Free 800 101 2657 (Singapore)
Toll Free 1 800 81 7340 (Malaysia)
orders.singapore@partridgepublishing.com

www.partridgepublishing.com/singapore

Preface

All time summer!! Baby....

These are what we, Malaysians could actually hear from tourists that walked us by.

For me, I personally think Malaysia is one of the coolest places in the world, though there are so many wonderful tropical countries in the world. I always feel Malaysia is special in terms of the multicultural delight dishes, buildings, industries and even people here.

I just love the mixture and combination of those artistic multi-coloured elements.

Not just that, the most awesome part is it is summer at all time although there may be raining seasons and yet accompanied by terrifying thunderbolt. Despite that, the sun will always brighten our days throughout the years.

I just think that what if the sun's beam that slants through the window in the bedroom, can no longer keep you warm while you just wake up from your sleep; what if you don't get to walk on the street with just a T-shirt on as it is going to freeze you to death by way of doing that? All of the sudden, everything around you changes without expecting it. It just happens with no warning?

Frankly, I also love how winter time would make me feel where the snowflake falling into places which cover everything in white. I always imagine that how the snowflake would melt on my hand. I always wonder whether is it possible or not to happen in where I live. I just love how winter would thrill me.

However, if I really have to live in winter at all time..... I would not know what to do...................... All I know is as I grow older, I realise sometimes you might not know how precious the particular thing is until you lost it.........

So, I still think to feel proud in telling the world where I came from in spite of the tarnished name in the eyes of the world.

MY HAPPILY LONELY BIRTHDAY

4/12/2000

1 She has always been the one and only

'Angela, Happy Birthday!'

This is what grandma said in this morning. The birds on the tree branches started to sing like nightingales. So, she wondered if it was a competition. It was when the eyelids were first opened. There she goes again. She was found laying on the bed like a corpse.

Her filthy eyes were on the window. This was observable. It was a moderately thick mist swirling around the hill in the backyard of the terrace house. She then realised it was still in the starting point of the day. It was not just cold, but it also made the eye sight became blurry.

She was just curious that where the mists came from. A research was conducted on the mystery previously. However, an obligation was occurred. She knew she had to ask her science teacher in school. This is how she always does.

An elucidation was heard and she could remember here. As she said, it is mainly because of the reduction of the surrounded temperature. This has made large number of tiny drops of warmer double H and an O element in the sky to be rapidly cooled.

A conversion will be tracked down. The originally invisible gas into tiny visible double H and an O droplet. It is really amazing!! What nourishes the natural phenomena has composed a beautiful musical landscape.

That makes her even more curious about the formation of snow. This is because of the hard work for a long wait of harvest. She still tries, even now, to dream of how does it like if she could be at a white land with both of them. She had even thought of staying in that land with them.

Nonetheless, she knew it was not the reality. She always thinks about the reason why Malaysia is not in the list of distinction. It may not be her faculty to find this out. She still rewinds the question when no one else remembers. Sometimes, she really hopes it would snow here. Despite that, it is why she will usually lay on the bed even if she already wakes up from a long night dream.

This is also what grandma used to tell her. She found it as a task like the decision has to be made between what to wear for the outfit of the day. As the explanation was told. She just feels warmer in the bed in the morning which is full of cold moist and so, that is the fundamental cause??

It is whereby she always gets to go to school on time. I mean, exactly on time. Everybody in her class knows her 'hidden talent'. It can be said that it is rare to see what is unusual to her. Perhaps, to be exact, I should say it never happened.

She can actually see the primary school she currently studies, when she stands on the balcony sometimes, and stares at the red sky. Due to this convenient rationale, grandma will always accompany her to go to school in the morning. It will be the same in spite of the good or the bad, she picks her up. There is how the journey begins. Isn't that lovely??

She doesn't know why but it just comes across in her head. Awkwardly, something has become so different today. An extra tuition class was offered to attend today. While they were still on their way walking to school, she secretly held her head and peeped. It is not easy for grandma in the period of not more or less than six years. The only member has still been here all the time in this lonely journey.

It is a cruel thing to know. A witness of the revelation. The pretty wrinkles around the blue eyes will always catch her eyes. It is how she starts capturing freckles scattering around her cheeks. This is simply adorable. She then laughs. So, a mutter was heard, 'I love you, grandma'. When a doubt was appeared, she just giggled and the question was left unresolved.

She really could not know why the supposed response was given like that. All she can feel in it is a sufficiently magnificent love. It is always about these two little ordinary persons. She would actually forget to breathe when she was gone out of sight.

2 The monster that haunted over

Flashback was done. The moment about she entered the class for the first time. It was her first year in primary school. Before she entered the room, the intentional noise made were polluting the tranquil morning. She then heard, a request from grandma to walk into the class by her own.

She just clung to a long, rough hand so tight; the respite palms were sweating; the clammy heart was beating loudly and she stopped taking in for a second. It is because the storm. That was a new place after the cruel disaster. There were numerous strangers in that place. These eyes in the class were on her like she was an unwelcomed alien.

She tried to bargain with the adult so that she would be brought home right away. However, she insisted for the little one to go in. She said if that vulnerable height remembered how a good girl does. All she needed to do is taking the courage to face what has been appreciated of fear the most.

I guess she hopes her grandchild to know what is the real meaning of being independence, and hence the uncertainty will not be relied on that much.

The time of before Angela started learning to count her fingers was reminded. She stayed in an orphanage during that time. Before that, she knew her parents were received a permanent pernicious summon to heaven. She was the solely lucky one in that terrific car accident. It really startled the dying beats; it was at the age of four. She behaved so weird in the aftermath of the tragic.

It was like her voice had not been heard for long time as she just wanted to deviate from the adults' attention. It was the place she should not step in. It seemed so wrong to be there. She still felt the existence of her parents. She wanted to go back to her family house that they all stayed.

However, those strange officers just grabbed her here. She did not volunteer for this. She was so mad. She really did not want to start a communication with people there as a defiance of the involuntary decision. The condition was exacerbated. She could see what they called delusion. They said she heard the beckons from the heaven were alive. She started talking with those voices, at the same time, she dreamt about the reality.

She could still recall the dream. It just kept repeating in the big head whereas she could not find any replay button. The real scene was brought in the nightmare happened long time ago.

She saw stream of blood covered by various pieces of broken glass in the front driver and passenger seats there. Nobody was found in that place. This was the moment she lost sanity without any acknowledgement about what was devotion. She even fell sick seriously as a consequence of staying up at the time where nobody does.

It was a strong affection of the torturing giant indecent monster. And yet, it was a battle. She was retrieved that she would never get over it. She was circumagitated by the speed of light with just laying on the bed of the orphanage.

Nevertheless, one day, it was when she was once regaining conscious in a turbulent state. A black shadow was sensed moving constantly in front of her, touching her hand and telling her to stay alright. Suddenly, a harsh voice shocked her and 'the shadow' by saying 'Azlina, what're you doing?'. It all went black again.

3 The heart-warming one

She is not sure whether it was merely a dream or not but the nihility was appreciated as genuine; the touch was keeping her warm for a moment. After she got a chance to open the irksome eyes, she noticed there were bundles of the paper folded goose right next to the bed.

It was out of curiosity. She was just unfolding the'gooses', and only realising it was a girl who named 'Azlina' and tried to send all the best wishes to her by making all these sweet 'gooses'. Nowadays, she still keeps the 'gooses' as she wishes to say the preciously rare to her personally one day. However, she does not know when her desires will be fulfilled.

The very last time Azlina was tracked was when she was still laying on the bed like a literally sleeping vampire. Seriously, she would even get shocked until now when she looks into the mirror sometimes. She looked hideous.

It was so heart melting. What a stranger would do for you. That's what she always thinks. A person that Angela never met again so far in life. It is an invincible mark in her heart. She knows for sure. This girl is definitely someone special to her who makes her feel different even though she is just someone who only existing in the wonderland. All she heard as to the unknown special friend was she was adopted by a middle-aged couple living in Johor Baharu. She tried many ways to reach her out, but it was not something she pictured.

It is just like searching a needle in the deep blue ocean. She also wrote letters to her until now. The outcome is a little bit disappointing. There was no any supposed news.

A few months later, the local council managed to make contact with grandma. She was used to live alone in the broad multi-habitual puzzle. The dreadful news was heard. She then flew all the way from her hometown to Penang with a broken heart. She decided to stay in Penang. It is which was the island the big head was born.

Grandma might think she knows nothing but it is wrong. She knew. Grandma was worried. The little one was still weary at that time and it might not be probable to travel away from the island.

An advice was provided by the smart alecks. Complete recovery is hard. However, lack of changes on the surrounding environment is necessary. Whenever she was reminded of, she held her tears back. She knew the negative melancholy melody haunted her down inside. It was long time ago when the wicked joke took over.

Grandma is someone she will look up for. Perhaps, a role model. She will do the same in return for the broken one. Nevertheless, guess what grandma was told. She smiled as she always does. She claimed she simply fell in love with the multi-coloured culture of Malaysia. It made her impossible to leave.

What she said is true. I think. We don't indulge in tyrannical racial scandal. We love each other. No discrimination. The diversity on our appearance does not make the inner element of unity to lose its priority. However, she knows it's beyond of what she was informed.

Since then, grandma became the guardian in legal mean. She also automatically became the personal family trustee. Whatever it is left, it will still go to the little one, even the house they are living right now belongs to those in the heaven. After all, it is just a small terrace house in a residential area.

It is painted in white. As she wished, Angela's favourite colour. There is a place outside the house which allows grandma to perform her skilful gardening talent on it. She cultivates the youth. Specifically, grandma loves daisy. She just loves its simplicity when she sees the small wild flowers with only white petals and a yellow centre.

'Aren't they beautiful?' The question she always asks without any reply.

She remembers, 'Although people do not usually put their attention on them, they make other glow.' She knows that she is a sunflower lover. She hereby plants them among the humble. She says it will always be kept in mind of the role of a secret guardian when she looks at these plants.

4 The creepy house

Under the perfect weather, they were walking back home with wordless musical sound. They did not talk much but just listen to the noises appeared in the surrounding street. As usual, she always has the disturbing feeling whenever she has to walk pass by one of the houses. The said house is located at the corner of the street.

It seems like nobody is living in the house. The painted wall is diminishing. The grass grows wild over the abandoned garden. She never seen anyone walking out or in from the house. Grandma would cease the conversation when she just started to ask. She could not help herself from looking towards the house. It is a myth in the small town.

After they came back from school, she was brought to the kitchen. I guess she wanted to show the one year older girl about the cake she baked. The attention was then put on the nicely wrapped up gift beside the cake. The shape of the gift was regular and it was moderately bulky. A few of speculations were attempted but failed.

She originally thought it was a hand held mobile phone. Perhaps, something newly impressive. However, she did not see what she thought. It is a diary. It is never a prosaic. She said it is hand-made. She saw the sketches on the cover of the diary. She then asked 'Why does it look so familiar?'

She was told to think and figure out herself. She was thinking of whether she was hit by amnesia. No clue was appearing at all. Despite that, there is a pen inserting in between the holes of the diary's hard cover which prevents the diary to be accessible without taking off the pen.

Grandma said, 'It is time to let it all out. You can write as much as what you hear in the tiny room there.' All I know is that she knows her pretty well. It is a chance given to improve the weakness.

There is no any unexpected birthday wishes or the desired presents. She is still feeling happy. It is because it is enough for her to feel satisfied for the day.

THE LONG-LOST DOLL

17/12/2000

1 These holidays have been a deceiving one???

She has been going to that place. The place where everybody has to be very serious at all time. This has already been few weeks. The reason she has to wake up early. The extra effort they provide. It is purported for those who are going to fight in the final battle. You might have known though you are not here. It is necessary for all of us across the country to go through this breath taking process. She knew it is the only way before they could proceed further.

In other words, it is more like a legitimate obligation to her. However, there are not many of them dealing with it in the same way. I do feel different. It is not just a test on the things we have learnt in these six years. It is a spell to us.

It will then depend on how the outcome we can achieve. Some people may think it is not good to diversify all of us according to the results we get. It is heart-breaking to see how some of them are worn down. The spotlight will only appear on the smart.

However, she just thinks of the bright side. It might be because she has to do so. By way of dividing students into distinctive small groups, concentration can be focused on one whole group. Isn't it easier if it contains the same category by using the standardised method in delivering educational message?

Is it work for the sake of our better understanding? It is not really that bad, but it is more like assistance to her. I know everything has its angel and evil on each side. Whether there has been an overriding?

I guess this is how things work. Nevertheless, it is the last day today for her to complete the task. Her name is everywhere in the list. Grandma walked her back from school as usual.

Nothing special today. The scorching hot weather I remember; the hectic traffic on the road; the mobile food stalls I love as well as the conversation between pigeons found on the lamp poses squatting at the road side. Not to mention, the legendary 'spooky house'.

2 It is never too late to be right again

Grandma told her that they got to be hurry today on the ground of her plan for something to work. She asked her to guess on what was actually in the excited state of mind. The question came first even before Angela started to ask. She was running out of idea. What was coming up for the next moment was the hardest prediction. She just refused to say anything as she was too frustrated to know that it would just be another vain attempt again.

She pouted. Grandma thought she was mad at her but actually it was not. Instead, it was just another attention seeker. I knew it was running out of it during these few days. A speculation was then produced. She should be getting prepared of the stuffs. It has to be before we depart to visit an uncle living in Kuala Kedah, like we used to go ever since that time.

There she was again. It started with those you are familiar with. 'Easily getting frustrated was never a good habit that a good girl should have. It was the same when we were about to give up on something easily. Getting knocked down was not supposed to be an excuse.' She stopped here at this second.

Angela thought about it twice and then she apologized. Although she knew it was a bad habit, pestering was simply needed in this case. I guess Grandma has set a threshold for ages to be pampered. She just thought, 'Should she just accept the fact to redress her bad habits?' She had been walking but it was different this time. Her head was down for a little while.

Grandma tried to change the mode of the day. She was found patting her shoulder, by saying, 'My sweet darling, it is good that you realised what you have done wrong. So, it is never too late to make it right, girl.'

The smile she stared at and during this moment, she could even hear the flying fly. On the ground that she knew it would only be an evidence of your nose to the grindstone, if your action spoke louder than words.

3 This is what they usually don't do to start the New Year

Finally, they reached home after a short while. Angela did feel like there was no gravity at all when she was still having mathematic class in the school. However, the element of the exhaustion in her head was now like disappearing in the air. She would just describe this as preternatural in the sense that she did not even know why.

She was just lying on the couch there. Grandma saw her but noticed that she was not here. She just thought to comfort her laziness. Grandma just summoned her to walk out of her lazily comfort zone. It was the lunch time before they got started working on her unknown plan. She almost finished the lunch.

Grandma was walking unhurriedly with her both hands hiding at her back. Her eyebrows seemed a little bit frowned about the big head's response towards the surprise she was going to give.

Grandma first grinned and moved her right hand at a leisurely pace. She saw two pairs of glove. The missing puzzle was now clearly visible. The jungle in bald. She just wished to clean up their house right before the coming New Year. Extra spaces are needed for the new coming members to the room.

Therefore, Angela followed her back to go to the store room right behind the kitchen. She rarely went into the store room if there was no necessity to do so. She still remembers the last time she went in there was, when she needed to find her badminton racket which she did not really play the match in the end of the day.

The room was gloomy with weak sunlight slanting through the small gaps she saw in the window, as the window was fully blocked by the bulky cupboard. This cupboard was…….. It was…….. It was originally belonging to her late parents. It was initially placed in their room upstairs. It was a gift from the uncle living in Kedah.

That man was cherishing it as much as his wife. The design on the cupboard was literally not fitting the theme of the room that he wanted to decorate. He still put in his room. We all know what it was. That was what she could hear from her as she only knew this much from her mother, before she actually got married.

By knowing its importance, she seemed to understand why it is still here even though it looked slightly decayed from the last time she saw it. Despite telling the stories behind all the antiques found here, they started packing up the unwanted toys and books that she loved to read during her childhood time.

It was really funny as the small room looked obviously and distinctively larger. She spotted a whole big box of toys and dolls like teddy bear, her favourite Minnie and Micky, Donald Duck, Goffy and et cetera. She then moved them out of the room and squatted on the floor to take a closer look at these dolls one by one.

Amazingly, she could barely remember about the disney dolls. As they all were the presents from her dad's friends in her one years old birthday party. That's what she saw in the photo albums. It can be found in the drawer of her desk back in her room for all these time. She took them out one by one rigorously but it was still failed to avoid. She just thought to herself that they should get facial masks before the beginning.

She then sneezed. The stemutation had made the dust whirling all over the place. She saw a doll. It was Woody. The lighting was striking in her head. She was totally becoming empty at this time. The bloody cuttery had stabbed her straight into her heart. It was what to feel in the mincer. She was brought back to that place again.

It was in the year of 1993. She became a big fan of Indiana Tales animation on television since five months back. She loved the character of Woody. It was a girl who loved dressing up like a cowboy. She always thought she was so cool when she could save the whole world whenever someone evil wished to enforce some plans in bad faith. She was begging her parents so badly to buy for her when she saw it in a shopping complex.

Finally, they surrendered. They brought that cute little thing back to home. However, the happiness ended as fast as a sudden flash while they were in the car on their way back home.….

4 The bulky stone

The memory stopped here. She was crying on the floor. Grandma went out from the store room and put her in her arm. She knew what was wrong with her. She needed not to say any words. The fact is now clear. It was still there all the time even if you forgot about it sometimes. It was like a tattoo, with an ugly demon, as if you wanted to.

This was why she always felt heavy though she looked thinner than she was used to be.......

Grandma knew about its existence, just that she opted to pretend as she knew it was going to be ended up in this way. She was really scared of hurting the broken heart recklessly. Doctor Humar said to her once, this could be the toughest wound to be healed. It could be a cycle. Perhaps, scars make you stronger.

It would be absolutely normal for an adult to be caught in trauma. There would not possibly be an exception for a four years old child to get over the simultaneous and immediate loss of her affectionately love towards her parents. It would just follow you, potentially forever and ever, like your invisible friend.

She was getting calmer after soaking in peaceful silence for more than ten minutes. Grandma told her that the annual appointment made with Doctor Humar has reached its deadline. She might want to bring her over to his clinic in Tanjung Bungah there right before Christmas week.

She looked into the determinative eyes. She just did not want to fret her, though there were many peevish voices revolving you. She is just too tired to hold on, like she would be collapsing at any minute. She stared at her senescent cells on her face. She is definitely getting older. All she knows is that it is the time to turn it upside.

5 Just keep the sadness

Grandma just told her that she was going to give the boxes away to the orphanage. She was screaming in and out. She stopped her from giving away the particular doll, Woody. The doll which has everything that she wishes to remember and forget at the same time. She begged her to keep it in the store room.

Grandma kept quiet for awhile and then said yes. She stood there by watching her taking Woody away from her. The door was finally shut. It could be kept in the dark momentarily.

THE COLD SWEAT
YOU WERE BROUGHT INTO

20/12/2000

1 The beneficial seduction of the said amusement

She was unwilling to go to see Doctor Humar ever since the day Grandma mentioned about the appointment made three days ago. She did not really reject grandma's quest in the beginning. As she firstly did not want to disappoint the one with frowned eyebrows. It was because of the fact that she might get paranoid as she thought she was mentally in need of assistance.

She still refused to get into the circle in the outside world; she thought she might forget about it in latter time.

Unfortunately, she did not. She insisted that the big head should go to Doctor Humar's clinic there. He was the psychiatrist who was efficacious in treating illness among children. She said it was all for her own good. Furthermore, grandma thought that you could not just keep running away from your obligation. She was thinking to herself that, 'What obligation has to do with consulting a doctor? Granny. It is not my job to see a doctor!!'

She knew it was derived from good intention. However, she just felt awkward every time she went to his clinic. This feeling really made her felt uncomfortable. She remembers once when she walked into his clinic. There was a long queue right there in the waiting hall. People there gave a kind of gaze like she was an alien.

In other words, she always felt like she was being watched by the people in the unfamiliar place. This was exactly like she was first entering the class during her first year in the primary school. It really made her wanted to leave the place as soon as possible.

The feeling she had about herself had disgusted her the most. She would also be embarrassed by her sweaty palm in a cooling environment like Doctor Humar's clinic. She would even feel afraid about shaking hands or touching other people, when other kids came up to approach her.

It was not because she did not like making new friend?!

She would still feel like away from the crowd even though she had been surrounded by a bunch of good friends. She just needed to even if she found it weird to do so. She just loved to be alone in order to get herself a clear picture.

The doctor that diagnosed her was good and kind. He was approximately at the beginning of the golden age. She did not mean to be rude but the salient peculiar really caught her eyes every time he talked. She just kept staring at his face with a question swimming in her head. She was wondering that why they were different in colours.

This was how she got distracted from the discomfort that she previously felt in the waiting hall. Besides that, she would feel getting drunk out of the musical intoxication due to the piano music played as the background music. The way he diagnosed her was easily conducted. He would just ask her to sit on the three person seats couch. She would see a well – prepared drawing paper and a crayon.

He would then ask her to draw something on the blank paper. She had figured out the purpose for this game about three years ago. As she heard from Lucas's explanation in medical term soon after she told him. This was why he always showed her his proud face. It seems like it was her bad that she did not want to believe he was the one who knew everything.

After half an hour of effort of drawing, he would dismiss her. Grandma would ask her to wait for her alone outside his office, and she would never find out what was behind the unopened door. Something bad or good??

She was left alone. She was found sitting in the middle of the hall while thinking about what grandma would have been told. The moment you get into the forest, you never knew which would be the right way. Grandma came out from the snooty room and talked to her. She was not responsive as still tried exploring the depth of the ocean. Nevertheless, it would just be a disappointment as she would never get an answer every time she asked.

She would just keep shaking her head by telling that, 'Everything is alright, the little one. I have everything in control.' She just said like she never knew how she would be kept awake all night. In order to ease the anxiety, she would just try to capitulate whatever was on her mind like an abandoned puzzle game, when you could not figure out an answer for the chanciness.

She seemed to be awaken from a long dream while she heard her grandma calling her name repeatedly. She then replied, 'I am alright, grandma.' She asked with unsureness, 'For sure?? But why you kept grumbling with your untenanted eyes? It really scares me off, darling. Please don't ever do that again!'

She just answered her with a smile on her vexed look…..... She then told her that they could go for picnic at sea side in Batu Ferringhi. It was just in the vicinity of the clinic after the meeting with Doctor Humar. By having heard what she said, it was really thrilling when she was reminded of the potential fun we could actually have later.

2 The departure of partial enthusiasm

Before she went out very early this morning, grandma had got everything prepared for the purpose of her primary intention. Nevertheless, she still made some sandwiches which contained your favourite slices of cheese and eggs in small pieces. It was really speechless. You never knew how delicious it was like nothing would be stopping you from eating until the plate was becoming empty. She just thought, 'Is because of who we really are?'

I guess it is what we called magic. In spite of the food to be brought for picnic, she would wonder how they would get there. Grandma is not a recognised citizen. All of her relatives and friends are still living in the puzzled land. She never had a valid driving licence. So, she speculated they would go there with the way like they were used to.

The mind of plan to go taking the test for a legitimate licence until now, but it was only an unrealised plan. She always has daily hectic schedule. Furthermore, when she was still much younger, home alone was never a thing she would risk. It was causing her goose bumps when she thought of potentially physical and mental danger.

Moreover, it was not convenient to bring her along anywhere she went. Sometimes, she did look like the orchid flower in the garden. She was being cultivated rigorously indoor to prevent the glass made heart from damages. However, it has appeared more like a burden to grandma.

Apparently, grandma would be like getting paranoid when she was away from her for only hours. I remember once, when it was at the age of nine, she got an urgent call. It was from the international airport in Penang here,….... if I was not mistaken.

At first, I did not know what it was all about. Grandma just asked her to stay still from where she was. She assured her that she would be right back in a few hours. She just ran out of the door speedily like wildly strong wind in winter, I guess. She did not even say goodbye to her. I thought it must be something under tightening pressure.

So, she was just sitting on the couch while watching her favourite cartoon show – Indiana Tales. It was really heart –teasing on the ground that she wanted to force herself to look back the past. The melancholic fear in her earlier life though she did not want to remember. She knew avoiding would never help in healing nor enhancing.

Suddenly, she heard someone knocking the front door of her house. At this moment, she just thought grandma must have forgotten to lock the front gate and someone just got in and knocked the front door behind the couch. Perhaps, it might be grandma who had been forgetful all the time. She thought grandma did not bring the house key and so she had to knock the steel gated door so violently.

Nonetheless, 'One step forward, two steps back.' So, she was trying to dawdle. Every step she walked was little with her head leaning forward. She wished to check out who was standing in her front door, but at the same time, she was battling with fear.

Based on this reason, her limbs were suddenly like paralysed by the aggressive noises made by the person standing at the front door. She could barely move though she could still try to walk laboriously.

She could not believe what she just saw. It was something violent red standing in front of the door and waving through the gaps found in the door. She tried to scream but there was no sound to be made. She was boggling on what was in front of her.

By cooling down the anxiety, she tried to turn her back on that 'red' and run as fast as she could, but it was like a black magic. Something kept tilting her towards the front door. She wished to go backward but she walked forth instead.

She tried to scream for help with great effort. Unfortunately, she was muted forcefully. When she reached the front door, she saw someone standing and waving towards her but it had disgusted her badly. The person was looking like a living bloody zombie.

As she could see wounds all over his face and limbs, these opened slits had made him looked mucky. The smell of blood –stained shirt had suffocated her the most, as if there was no oxygen in the space she was standing currently.

She even heard that person muttering her name while he was trying to reach her hand through the steel gated door. She was flapping her hands as if they were her wings, in order to preclude the bloody contagious hand from touching her. However, he eventually still grabbed her arms.

She saw that she was drowning in the water. She could no longer breathe and therefore close her eyes with fatigue........

When she opened her eyes, she thought, 'Grandma!' Grandma's face leaning toward her face whereas she started to realise that she was lying on the couch. She was looking anxious and solicitous with her eyebrows frowned while her hands were holding her skinny arms. She seemed to get herself clearer in the next few minutes by regaining conscious.

Grandma just held the big head in like she thought she would never see her again. She just kept asking her questions like she did not remember who you were. She was mumbling for the whole day while no one seemed to understand what she was talking about. She finally understood those words expressed after some struggling in the hard way.

Grandma was going to airport to see her biological younger sister. I mean truly blood – related though I don't believe the fact until now. Let's get back to the story. Auntie Susie was keen to cure the feeling of hunger. So, when she went to a restaurant in the airport, she tended to lose attention over her luggage as she smelled food.

She therefore lost her luggage, which she put her thousand millions worth jewellery in it. The officers in the airport originally could not find where could the luggage be taken.

They were searching thoroughly all over the place. They were still not giving in their effort in searching when grandma reached there. In the meanwhile Auntie Susie was groaning about the security in the airport. Half an hour later, a service staff came up to Auntie Susie and said, 'I am so sorry, Miss Jacob. Am I right??'

Auntie Jacob replied surprisingly, 'Oh my god!!! It is mine!!! Thank you so much for finding it.' The staff looked stunned to observe her appreciation while replying her, 'You are the most welcome. It is our job to find the thing you lost in our airport. Can you please check whether there is anything missing inside your travel luggage?'

Auntie Susie opened her luggage right away. She was wary enough to flip through the things inside the bag. Everything was finely placed in the bag. Nothing got lost. The staff started to explain how it was transformed to a dramatic misunderstanding. The cleaning service crew thought it was something left by the customer out of recklessness. She then took the bag to the customer service.

They tried to search on the face of the bag for the contact number of the owner but failed. Ten minutes back from now, one of her colleagues, came to her and asked whether they had received any lost and found item in the customer service department. So, she just thought whether the bag could be belonging to…..

Stuffs like that had been revolving around you for the whole day. Grandma never left her alone in the house ever since that day, just because she thought the shadow of devil was still waving its hand towards her….

This was also the reason why they don't see a vehicle in the house. Therefore, she had called a taxicab as usual. The taxi driver was the one we got to know for the reasonably longest period, ever since she first came to Penang in order to take over the mess left behind by those in heaven.

He, Uncle Sahmir was the first taxi driver who brought her to the orphanage home Angela was staying. Grandma had continued dealing with him ever since the self-introduction was proposed. He is automatically efficient. He has been our family personalised taxi-driver for years. A very special guy to me. He does not speak much. He will only answer when you initiate the conversation….

He came five minutes before the actual time they needed to depart today. The appointment was made at 10 a.m. They started travelling on the road at 9 a.m. The sky was extremely clear today as she could barely see the cloud in the sky. It was like a beautiful bait to those inquisitive eyes before she got into the taxicab.

The sunlight shined through the soundly mind. It was like the moonlight before breaking dawn when she was walking back to her house from school on that day. She wished she could open the window of the car to touch the sun beam but grandma stopped her. The traffic was quite smooth today before they actually arrived at the clinic.

The clinic opened at 9.30 a.m. It did seem a little different from the last time you came here. She spotted the slope right beside the staircase with the handrails at the side. The wall was changed from white colour to light blue colour. It seemed more like an unfamiliar castle to start an adventurous day.

However, whatever new things she saw, she could never get rid the thrilling plan of her mind. She kept thinking about it from the second grandma revealed it during that time. She just could not wait for it anymore. There was going to be an eruption of joy and enthusiasm at any time.

In spite of the cheerfulness, she could only see a few kids sitting on the wooden chairs with their parents accompanying them. At this moment, she stared at grandma for awhile. She abruptly heard the young female nurse calling delicately, 'Angela.' It seemed nothing identical this time. Grandma walked through the door together with her.

As usual, she sat on the new sofa as she could tell from its appearance. Doctor Humar asked to draw something which first popped out in her drunken mind on a piece of drawing paper with a crayon. She did what he said while thinking about the picnic that she promised. She followed what he said but nothing was taken seriously.

I thought everything should be alright. He just smiled at them and the nurse requested them to go to the counter outside for the payment. She felt relieving as the moment you had been waiting for, had finally come. After the cash out, grandma just pulled her right hand as she is used to dawdle, sometimes.

They were heading to the place she covenanted after they got into the taxicab. After another half an hour trip, they eventually reached Batu Ferringhi. She thought she was too lucky today as the sky was looking similar as how her heart seemed like right now. The sky seemed like the mirror on the sea though there were clusters of cloud bejewelling with the dazzling sun beams.

3 It should be a good day

She could actually feel the fresh and salty breeze rustled her hair. The fallen leaves were whirling in the wind from far. People at the beach side were running back and forth. In fact, they were having fun. Some of them were lying on the sand, just to enjoy sunbathing. Some people were swimming in the blue warm water.

Everything was so nice today. I bet it was going to be a great day for them. She shouted to grandma, 'All time summer land!!!' Angela pulled her hand again in order to walk in a brisk pace. She first laid a piece of the white cloth on the softly rough sand and then only place all the foods and drinks on the cloth. So, she started running wild around the beach with the grant of the counterfeit liberty.

After half an hour of hide and seek game with the black shadow following your footsteps, she finally felt tired. It was weird to feel as if she was hiking uphill for a long time. She walked back to where grandma sat at. She was having the sandwiches she made at the very early morning. She took a deep breath like it was lack of oxygen to breathe in before talking. She then told grandma her wish to go playing at somewhere near the sea water.

Grandma stared at her for a few second. She looked like she was travelling backward somewhere farther from here. She thereby speculated that she was thinking about the thing told by Doctor Humar today. While she was doing the same thing as her grandma did, but she decided to be initiative.

She said that it was alright to go playing in the sea water but she kept reminding the only grandchild not to go to the deeper place for an eleven years old girl like her. She said waves and sea tide were senseless. They would pay you no feeling of sympathy and leaving you pled for some voluntary contribution of compassion.

She just swore to her that she would take good care of Angela. She then ran to the narrow side of the sea water. Grandma was watching. She was playing the sea water with her feet. It was like kicking the water molecules until they were vibrating unevenly. She was enjoying over the miracle her feet made in splashing unintentionally like a natural based fountain.

4 The cold sweat of mine??

Suddenly, the scene in front of her eyes had turned dull. She looked up to the sky. The sky was covered with angry clouds. It looked like the tears dropping moment could just be unstoppable. People in the sea was rushing back to the beach. At the same time, she heard grandma shouting on the beach from a mile away, 'Come back to the sea shore, QUICK!!'

While she was about to walk forth toward the sea shore, she heard someone yelling at her back. She turned her head around to clear the insecurity. She saw someone sinking inconsistently into the water. That person was like being pulled down into the water but he was struggling to go up to the surface again. He then gulped air with his mouth widely opened and shouted, 'SHARK!!!'

The scene was frozen in the place where she was standing. Grandma was trapped in the sea of frightened heart. She wished to move back to grandma's arm as soon as possible. It was in the sense that she knew it was extremely highly life risking if she was still there like an implanted tree with strong root underneath the sand in the water.

At the same time, she also wished she could go to the poor guy who was just in the short distance of where she was standing. She also wanted to save him from the bloody lethal mouth. However, the worst was that she was caught in between the inappropriate conflicts at the improper timing. Her timid shell could barely move.

The life guard was then carrying a sharp blade and walking steadily closer to the deadly sounded rhythm. Grandma wished to come over to grab her out from the heaven like purgatory but she was precluded from going further by the other life guard on the sea shore.

The life guard with his fighting weapon started swimming toward that unlucky's thrashing.....

He first dived into the water, and she later saw reddish blood pooling the blue water. A large fin was forcefully appearing on the water surface. The figure was trying to push the life guard away. The fearless guardian was stabbing directly on its controlling system. The ending seemed to be satisfying.

The unwelcomed purgatory's trooper had been defeated by the guardian who did not know how to define what was timorous. It is because he looked as he was. He then held that person's head up while swimming back to sea shore. She felt relieved now. She started to move forth. Grandma ran to her and held her so tightly.

She then walked to the beach where everyone was standing in a circle. She told grandma to check out how was that person now. She went near and heard them talking. The unfortunate one said feebly, 'It was a deadly shark with smooth back and a large fin on its back. These were the battle wounds found on my leg when it was sinking its teeth into my left calf. It would have dragged me down if you did not get here on time. I would lose in its hunting game. All I know is thank you.'

She turned her eye-sight to the bloody wounds. It was like many small slits with blood coming out from it. It did seem like a piece of formidably sewing art to her. She heard the thunder's warning for a sudden. She then looked back to the sea again. The sea tide was getting highly active until you saw the land was intruded.

The fretful heart was urging her to go back home right about now. She looked more exhausted unlike the one she saw this morning. She knew it was all because of the bumpy surviving intention they all saw just now. She said, 'Alright.' She held her hands tight and got back to the taxicab. Before the car started going forward, she turned her head back again to the crowd surrounding the unfortunate but the luckyest one for the dreadful day. 'Hope you will be alright.'

Indeed, it was the terrific race between the shark and that guy. Her palm was wet. She wondered, 'Is this the sweat from my palm or her palm??'

5 A sign of calling for help

Finally, they had reached their house. She helped grandma to move all the stuffs back to the house. Grandma saw the vacant sights and hence wondered if she was alright. She just expressed the question spinning around the enormous space. She asked, 'I just don't understand why. Why shark would appear here?? I thought our sea in Malaysia were free from shark.'

Grandma replied with a question mark, 'Everything happens for a reason we might not know. It is too large in scope for nobody like us to explore …..'

She guesses this is just another question that will haunt her for the night.

THE FABULOUS YEAR BEFORE
THE NEW YEAR

<u>31/12/2000</u>

1 The brand new definition of hardworking

Grandma always asks out of curiosity: What she has written in the faded pages of the diary book. Well, Angela always replies her with incongruous answers every time she asks her, such as, 'Nothing!'; 'Oh! Just something humorous about my school life!', or sometimes, she just said that, 'I still have not written much yet.' perhaps, 'I am just too hardworking to be lazy.'

The holy diary remains implausible for contact purpose. She knows her right to privacy will not be invaded, but who knows what might accidentally happen in latter time. This is the significant reason. She doesn't really like to make diary writing as her daily routine. A huge dislike for the feeling of being understood by others either the intention to explain when people don't understand.

It is just like the more people understand who you are, the lesser dress you are wearing. It is really uncomfortable to compromise with the feeling. Speaking of that, she got reminded the time when she was in the second year of her primary school year. I can never forget how she was driven insane just because of this discomfort, internally self – disgusted thought.

On the first day to start the week, she went to school as usual with the companion of grandma. However, she was left alone to continue the journey ever since the beginning of her second year. She was walking alone to her class from the front gate in school.

It was because she wanted a mind training. She was demanded to be more independent. 'You have to grow up someday.' However, she never knew that, 'It is too hard for me to say goodbye to you!'

When she was about to go into the class, she saw something like a class meeting session. There were students gathering in a group in the center of the class. Their voices were intermingling in her ears but she could still hear what they were talking about. Archani was saying, 'Is it real that she is an orphan?'

'I don't know because that's what I heard from my friends in other class.' Malvin said. Shamirah interrupted, 'I also heard people saying that she used to live in an orphanage home. Her parents died out of a blood cuddling road accident many years ago.'

From what was heard, she just went mad. She yelled intensively loud, 'How could you all talk about my history like having a tea time cookie??? It is my business, not your business whether I am an orphan or not!!!!!'

She was really out of her mind at that moment. She ran out of the class immediately after shouting at them. They all looked innocently curious that the reason why behind all these dramatic shouting. As this was something fresh in the class. She was nobly known to be a very quiet person. In the earlier years in primary school, she did not really talk much and make many friends as how she should have done that in the class.

2 The wall of insecurity

She just kept running straight right to the end of the walkway. She then stopped. You could hear her breathing convulsively as if she was drowning. At the same time, she kept seeing the scenes of how the accident occurred like a reflection in the mirror. It was there all the time even if she might forget about it or perchance, when she was not really being reminded of.

It was inheritably terrible as she could still feel the close interconnection between them. It was really dismaying to think of how she became an orphan as well as the memory of loneliness to be in the orphanage house. She did not know how to overcome this strongly invincible monster.

She squatted on the floor, and then started crying silently with the hope that she could actually enjoy the melancholic moment alone here. I guess her fellow classmate, Lucas, who was the class representative at that time, had told the class teacher, Miss Lee.

She found Angela at the dead end of the corridor. She went up to her by calling her name gently. She patted the shaky shoulder delicately with her left hand. On the other hand, she laid her right hand on top of the timid right hand as she could feel her impressibly soft skin.

She tried to comfort patiently though she cried tremendously louder. It was as a result of the wish made to avoid hearing what she was going to say. After struggling in bringing her back to class for two hours, the effort was paid off. She just followed the class teacher walking to the class at her back. The students in the class were looking at her.

They looked suspicious. I guess they were figuring out what was the culprit of driving her into the state of madness. Most of them stood up simultaneously and walked to her direction. They were apologizing about their conversation which made her felt bad. Shamirah explained that it was purely a misunderstanding.

On the ground that, they were just talking about the dramatic story show on the channel of TV3. They did not know about her real life story until today. Lucas seemed to know a lot about her. He explained well to the rest about her hypersensitive nature. The funny thing is about, she was called as an universal perilous girl ever by a guy, who named Jun.

She was mad but feeling hilarious at the same time every time he did that. She would not have a valid reason to get angry at him even though he still addressed her as the universal perilous girl ever whenever he saw her walking along the corridor. However, the ending for that day was quite dramatically marvellous. I remember.….

'Now, we know. I am so sorry to say thing that stimulated you badly. We did not mean it.' Archani said. She was not complacent and apologizing shamefully by saying, 'It is my fault too. I should not have made a big fuss on innocent people like you guys. I am sorry.' They seemed to forgive her madness. They were smiling at her and giving a group hug . . .

I guess this unpleasant incident had demolished the wall existed between her and her classmates. They became closer friends though she still preferred to be the weirdo in their eyes. She still loves sitting at the corner there to do her own thing while others are mingling well with each other and playing games.

I guess this is the reason why she is still seeing Dr. Humar.

3 Her favourite song ever!!!

It was a tiring journey to travel on the road for three and a half hours continuously yesterday. Grandma decided to take her back to her late father's hometown in order to visit her father's godfather. She was found extraordinarily exhausted. It was joyful but she just finished celebrating Christmas five days ago.

She just thought of getting some naps after lunch in the consecutive days while enjoying the music grandma bought for her as the Christmas present this year. She was totally surprised by the gift she bought this year as she kept it all too good as a holy secret without her knowing.

Normally, no secret can be hidden from her sharpening eyes. Nevertheless, she was laughing at her own failure this time.

She used to spend her free time at home by listening to radio. She was not the type of enjoying to go to public places even though grandma was around. If she did go, she would not stay long.

Let's go back to the music. She had been addicted to the band of M2M for quite awhile. The group was a fantastic pop music duo formed by two Norwegians, namely Marion Elise Raven and Marit Elisabeth Larsen.

She was particularly in love with one of their song, titled 'Pretty Boy'. She would always wait in front of the radio for the whole day if she could. It's just for the song to be played in the radio, so that she could actually rave against the rhythms of the song like crazy. It was nothing newly strange to grandma.

A few days back, she wished to unwrap the present right after the dinner grandma cooked during Christmas Eve but she was precluded from doing that. She requested that no unwrapping the presents was ever allowed but only after tonight. She seemed a little bit down and pouted as she always did whenever she did not get what she wanted.

She went to the bed room in order to sleep early, so that the time would pass her by a little bit faster. Screaming inside out to yourself that no patience could be tolerated to wake up in the morning on the next day. She bounced backward onto her bed and tried to get herself become sleepy. Unfortunately, it did not work.

She was rolling thoroughly right and left on the bed the whole night.

Finally, a last long breath was taken in deciding to get up from the bed in order to cure the seed of sickness sowed in her heart. She sneaked out of her room and went down the stair while grandma was still sleeping in her room.

It was all done in still. She tried to reach her hand hither to the presents that were placed underneath the Christmas tree.

However, she still stood and mulled for a long time, though, in fact, only a few minutes passed by. She walked closer towards the presents painstakingly as what was she doing did not seem right to her. After the civil battle, she just could not hold the devil inside any longer.

She unwrapped the present aggresively in slow motion, as she was too excited about her incriminating intention but she wished to offer disguise.

It was a M2M ALBUM. She raved in silence. It felt like she was much more elated than winning a grand prize in the national lottery. She just knew that there would not be any other person who would actually treat her as attentive as grandma did. She was then feeling giddy as she was quite sleepy at this late of night.

Grandma did not say anything about this as she noticed that the mess she did to the floor was all cleaned on the next afternoon.

The way she pampers will make her harder to survive alone.

4 They looked almost the same!!!!

Talking about festival seasons, it was New Year's Eve today. She was now at god grandpa Kok's house in Kuala Kedah with grandma. They reached here by bus yesterday. It was a long journey though it was not that time-consuming indeed. Uncle Kok picked up them from Terminal Bus Station where they were dropped at.

It was not the first time for our eyes to meet. It was ambiguously pleasant. She could barely remember that before her dad passed away.

They went to his house for the sake of celebrating Chinese New Year when she was still four or perhaps three years old. She could still find some photos in the album to incorporate what had been remembered.

He looked cute because of his small body. I also love his friendly, confident, wide smile with the decoration of beard. The way he spoke was also wreathed in smiles. He is special. That's all I know. Something inside of him charms you and you just know what it is.

He lived all in the lonely bungalow as big as the field in her primary school. He said he could only see his sons and daughters during the visit once a year, mostly during Chinese New Year. He already got used to the life like this in the maze.

He told, many people were wondering why he insistence of the accompanied choice. The thought he had of avoiding the restriction of the choice of life of his own as well as others. The mistakes he wanted to make it right again before the last breath but not just to fulfil his own desire.

He was an independent man indeed. He could take care of himself though he might ruin the perfect days in his life by way of the self-indulged infallibility of his insistency. From this point of view, she did think they looked almost the same despite the physical appearance, the way of thinking was so consistent.

She did not understand what did it mean. Nowadays, she finally resolved the incomplete puzzles. It just reminded her of the celestial memory while her eyes were on him. She also enjoyed conversing with him. It is because she could only know more about her late father through his story telling moment.

To him, his god son was a virtuous man. He would still be keeping in touch with him even if not much family left and the fact that he moved to Penang before the deadly car crash.

He did not know the fretful news until he went all the way down to Penang to visit him. As he wondered the reason why the last time he saw him was during the visit a year ago. The fate had also brought two of the wise together. Since then, they became good friends.

5 The colourful fire rain in the sky

Despite the story –telling session yesterday, he brought her and grandma to visit Kota Kuala Kedah and the museum here in the early morning right after the breakfast at a Mamak restaurant. According to our volunteer tour guide, Kota Kuala Kedah is also known as Kota Kuala Bahang. It is only located one kilometer from Kuala Kedah town.

Indeed, this is a classical ancient small town in Kedah. It did make you feel like how you felt in Penang but the life here was peacefully sounding in the downtempo footsteps. Along the way, by looking out of the window from the slow-moving car, there were boat builders and also a row of makeshift stalls at the roadside selling fresh and dried marine goods.

There was the Kuala Kedah Yacht Marina right beside the fort. Although it was not opened for public to visit, luckily, it did offer awesome opportunities for photo-taking. He also said the spotlight would be on Plaza Kuala Kedah tomorrow, right opposite the jetty where they could get all kinds of dried seafood as souvenirs, especially the one should not be missed, he stressed. 'The famous Kuala Kedah Belacan' (shrimp paste).

She thought it would be one of her favourite moment as she was reminded of the wishful requests by the friends at school.

She also loved the Thai cuisine he treated them at the Blut Corner there. She just could not resist the tom yam seafood though she was not the spicy challenger. The tourists there acclaimed that the tom yam was deserved a thumb up once you had a taste of the food in heaven. A target has never been missed.

They went hither to the new bench near the jetty as he said there would be a show later tonight. It was almost twelve o'clock. Before they actually sat on the bench facing the sea view, she heard a reasonably enormous explosion in the sky. She later saw the sky was filled with multi-coloured fire rain. The jaws dropped, 'Wow!'

The sky became brighter for a sudden. It was still eye-pleasing despite she had seen it for several times in different places. The fire rain was appearing with distinctive pattern like a staggering animation movie played in the sky. She really wished the show would not end tonight. However, it did not come true.

I guess the night could only continue illuminating in her dream tonight.

THE FAMILIAR TRACE

<u>4/3/2001</u>

1 Love at first sight?

Michael, who is one of her 'busy' classmates, on the ground that he is the class representative. He has the decent class teacher favourite look where he appears to be smart with the round – famed glasses on his chubby face and the moderately short and eight to two split, well-combed hair.

She just loves observing him walking in and out from the class. It is really one of the reasons to make a smile on her face. It is not an insult but aesthetic. It is fun to watch over people when they don't really notice you doing this to them. It is just something less than stalking people.

Seriously, he is cute. He is not just teacher favourite student and also their beloved leader in the class as well. He never learnt to say no to their quests. He was used to tell, 'He dreamt to be a superman once upon a time.' She just thought, 'Are we connected?'

He seemed to be a little bit of unusually excited today. He said to his best pal in the class who named Guna, 'I am in love.' You could tell the horrid effect on Guna. By raising his eye-brows, he just gave him the look like 'Are you okay?'. He continued to say 'For real? Who's the lucky one?'

Michael replied with his pearl – white like teeth. 'What a bright smile!' It reminded her of him ……. The only one thing she could picture about him after a long good bye….. Michael, he was like a three years old kid who got surprised by an unexpectable gift, as you could see his feet were not on the ground.

He was technically floating in the air though theoretically human cannot fly without any assistance of gadgets.

He told Guna that 'You know what? When I sent the homework we did to the teachers' office ………. I……. I ……I..I..I saw ….' He just kept breathing like he was at outer space. 'What is it?' Guna replied with a feeling of impatient.

Michael reverted to where he stopped, 'I saw an angel ….. with intriguing figure and her talking eyes. I bet that she got incredible long hair ever. She could make my heart stop beating with only the first sight. Seriously, I never felt anything like that. I guess, this is what we call love…………'

Mentioning about defining what is love. It may be too early for a twelve years old kid to illustrate, who is just beguiled by her irresistible beauty. I just know young affection gapes may not fit in inheriting, but I just think love should not be judged from what the eye-candy killing hook does to you. I don't know if it is true.

A dubious eternity I have been questioning. I guess Guna was also verbally influenced by Michael's description. He said to Michael that 'Who is she? Which class she is from? I would like to meet her in person.' Michael told Guna that it is the new girl from 6B. He just pulled Guna's hand and walked swiftly out from the class.

'New girl?' Based on what he said, she also felt like she should meet this girl. When she was about to get up from her seat and ready to go meeting this new girl, the class teacher stepped into the class and coincidently. Michael and Guna returned to the class and got back to their seats.

'Is it a twisted fate?' She was thinking about the new girl during the whole lesson. She was looking at her teacher but the mind was drifting to 6B. She doesn't know how but she just has a feeling that it's going to be something. She was too keen to know more about her.

2 Something about the girl

She was like a scurrying ant got trapped in a place that it does not belong to. She just wished to go out from the class. She just hoped the bell would ring in the next minute. She begged for it. She doesn't know why she felt like it was the longest science class she ever had. She never experienced stuff like that before. Today has been so extraordinary for her to encounter day-dreaming.

She was analysing about the ambiguous reason. 'Is it because of hearing what Michael said that made me felt that way; I like girls??! Or, perhaps, is it due to my adventurous curiosity? or she really means something to me?. A girl that I never met in person which made me undergone complication??' Its possibility is just like swallowing thirty-four inches wide of burger in just one minute.

She was staring at her teacher with an empty shell. She just kept teaching and explaining by waving her hands up and down. For that moment, she really thought the princess who looks so fair. It is like she is always glittering as a shining star in front of the blackboard. She tried to summon us for the sake of the sovereignty of knowledge without losing her sophistication.

She always dresses herself up in a long dress with a plain top. She will normally wear flat with small ribbons on them. She is impressively doing well with flat shoes because high heels will make her unreachable.

It was also noticed that she loves decorating herself in plain white dress. She simply looks like friendly harmless angel in the theatre. Angela doesn't seem to know why she always catches her vacant eyes. 'Is it because of it is my favourite colour too?'

She just loves the angelic one as her science student. As she is curious in everything, like almost everything, seriously, even grandma will sometimes feel annoying by reason of the way she keeps bugging her for an answer to her question, which is totally out of her capability.

When the curiosity starts to play its role for the day, the angel in the theatre will always give a logical intelligent statement for clarifying the doubt in a lovely tune. This really makes her frequently self-inquiring about the question. 'Is it a good thing or bad thing?' Nevertheless, it is still remained vague until today.

She was so concentrating on what she taught but it seemed like she was the only awakened one. The rest of them were mostly like mind flew over the cloud. She demonstrated why it does not snow in Malaysia. This reminded her of what grandma described to her when it was snowing in Australia. She said it was not just cold. It was something more than that.

She could really feel like the blood in her body was crystallizing into solid. She could barely walk on the thin sheet when the winter storm paid them a visit. Nonetheless, the naive age still thought it was so cool to experience freezing under sunlight. There would be no more sweating, the environment around you was painted in white. Everything would be looking theatrically and romantically simple in the imaginative picture.

She is staying in Malaysia for eleven years. She has never been beyond the boundary of this country. Thereby, due to the lack of actual geographical knowledge, she always wonders that could it ever happen in Malaysia so that she could go through a white New Year for only one time. She is not greedy, is she?

All she ever anticipated had happened. The bell finally rang. After taking a bow to thank her, most of the students in the class just ran out from the class and rushed to the canteen but meanwhile, for certain students, they just stayed in the classroom and enjoyed the foods were brought from home.

You? The very first thing to do in the list for fulfilling the space she had during this break time is……. Go to see that girl behind the rumour. The weary mind to think whether the unplanned greeting would be disappointing but she still wanted to try her luck.

3 It appeared again!

She quickly walked out from the classroom and went one floor up to 6B. She was creeping into that class so that no one would notice an alien intruder in that class. While she was whirling around in the classroom to search for that girl, she felt someone tapping her right shoulder for a sudden and saying 'What are you doing here, Angela?'

For that moment, she got shocked with the shivering shoulder. She turned her head around. She saw him….. 'Oh! It's you!! Hi, Lucas, long time no see and you still love scaring me with no warning.' He replied 'Hi, Angela. So sorry for frightening you. Are you looking for somebody? You look empty and blurry today.'

She really got surprised by his words. A friend who previously studied in the same class for only one year. He is presumably known as someone who knows her quite well. So, the story of the day was heard that she was looking over the new girl who just came in.

However, she was still let down by his reply that the girl she looked for had already gone away. She was a little too late, it would be a tough task to go to canteen and search for someone she never met before in the crowd.

Bearing that in mind, she just let the head down and those desperate eyes were on the ground. Her right hand was holding and scrubbing her left hand at the same time. She loves doing that with unknown reason. Weirdly, it really made her felt better. It was never in the list of encouragement. The outspoken and outgoing characters would never be enjoying priority substantially because of the melancholic tragedy.

She is used to feel difficult to express. It is not always coming from the mouth but through writing. She finds out not long ago, it is simply easier in clean hand. So, writing diary has been her habit that she can never ever get rid of. It was started since she got this precious present though she doesn't write as frequently as what is normally expected.

By eyeballing her disappointed demeanour for a few minute, he asked her to follow him for having meals in the canteen. He would show her where the girl was if the wish was an arrangement.

He never asked her the reason, but he just did what she wished. She really felt heart-melting to have a friend like this in life. Can't you find someone who will do anything to assist you without asking for more like another secret guardian for her, can you?

She never told him how she felt and just smiled. She then said to him 'Okay' with a hopeless face because she knew anticipation would only bring more disenchantment. He just held her small right hand and walked her to the canteen. It was well anticipated from the start. The bell rang again. Angela and Lucas went back to their classes separately.

When she stepped into the class, she saw something which she could never ever believe in. At this moment, she was nearly in the state of trauma. 'It's the "goose". Unbelievable!! the goose that appeared on my desk……'

THE NO. 2

1 The hope

This was just outrageous. It happened again. This seemed familiar to her. She still figured out whose the 'goose' belong to by staying up all night and thinking about it. She unfolded the 'goose' and hoped that there might be some clues to clear up the tedious ambiguity. She realised nothing but just an anticlimax.

She started to resolve this question in mind with small little things. She knows where a fully complete picture is comprised of trivial pieces that people often neglect. Therefore, interrogation was started with the people sitting around her desk. Hopefully, there would no longer be a shroud of mist. However, this was just another vain attempt.

While she was thinking about the solution with no clues, and then hopeless just joined in. Shamshir, who is sitting at the two rows distance far from her desk, went up to her and said, 'It was a girl. That's all I know.' He just walked back to his seat after delivering what he witnessed.

'A girl?!' He just mentioned a girl. A speculation could be done that he might not know that girl, so he addressed her as 'a girl', perhaps a stranger.......
Could it be the new girl?

The fiery fire was burning inside out. It caused her to lose patient. Someone that she wishes to meet for so long …… Someone she wishes to say goodbye to but she could not……..Someone that makes her to be indebted to for no real justification.

She never got to know Azlina but a peculiar connection was in existence that binds you and a stranger together. It was like someone you knew in previous life. That's definitely going to be something.

34

She does not know why but she knows it is going to be another component to the air she is breathing. It is wizardly absurd I am asking you how could it be sensible to bear this feeling towards a stranger in mind. It even sounds so ridiculous to have it in the first place.

The feeling towards the new girl was extremely strong. It was highly probable that she could be Azlina. She did not know what was in the scrumpy mind. She frowned and then finally made up her mind. She raised her bony hand to ask the class teacher for permission to go to washroom.

'It was a lie! It was a lie!' She kept repeating these words to herself. She did not know that she was out of nowhere to get the gut to tell lie. It was a groundbreaking surprise that she should not have done. Her original intention was to go lurking in the corner of the wall near 6B class, so that the mission of identification could be accomplished.

She quietly scanned for the new face for a few minute while their class teacher was distributing their assignment. 'Azlina Mohammed Jamil!' The teacher called. She was blurred by the sudden-welcoming expectation. It could be real. She, a non-familiar feature may be the goose's owner.

2 The dark force

Due to the ground of her nervous disposition, she shouted when someone was tapping her right shoulder at her back. Everyone in the classes were looking out from the window like something terrifying was happening. The teacher was creeping over the source of the scream with fear.

The person standing at her back was pulling her to an unlocked store room and hiding in the dark. She still could not speak at that time. The struggle was hard. Just that person was covering her mouth with its hand. She felt so scared at that time.

I thought this could be the ending of the nostalgic life. She wished she could fight against the great unlawful force but she was not strong enough to do so. She did her best to feign an illusion so that she would be going back to the normal situation. She should be at the rightful place. When she opened her eyes, it would be the time to wake up from prodigious dream.

That person spoke: 'Don't worry, everything's going to be fine. They're all gone.' Wait a minute, she recognised this voice. 'Lucas! It's you! Why did you scare me like that? I thought I would be ceased to breathe.'

'I saved you!' Lucas seemed unabashed to tell her. 'Okay, thanks though I really don't know how it works.' She became sarcastic enough to say this at this moment. 'Seriously, if they caught us wandering outside the class, we would be executed with no mercy shown.' Lucas explained.

'Well, thanks for everything. I need to go back to my class! I am out for a quite some time, the class teacher would feel worried about me.' She explained to him and insisted to go.

He said 'Wait, the time for classes is going to end soon! I thought you are desperate to meet that girl, aren't you?' Soon after he finished his words, the bell rang. They quickly sneaked out from the dark and Lucas brought her to his class. Lucas pointed at the new girl and said 'It's her! Her name is Azlina.'

3 The reunion

She had goose-bumps when she had an eyeball confrontation with her. 'Is she the one?' She was asking herself. The new girl smiled at her while she finished packing up her stuff. She ambled towards her and said 'Hi, I hope you still remember me, Angela.' She just grinned as she never knew about all of her shrewder instinctive feelings. She shook her heavy head before walking to the girl in the legend.

She started the story with a sentence, 'Hi, Azlina. Do you know me?' She just could not believe the fact that she just knew the long lost name without asking. Furthermore, she just did not understand that how could she be sure that she was not calling the wrong person.

The new girl just answered the posted question calmly, 'Of course I know you. I can never forget your big brownish eyes with the long eyelashes decorating the snow white face.'

She thought that the speculation should be correct and therefore she asked with full level confidence. 'So, you are "Azlina", aren't you? The one who made paper folded gooses for me. I remembered the time when I was laying on the deadly horrid bed in the Harmonic Orphanage Home.'

She replied, 'Yes!' She then said nothing at all. Her world was not sound due to the momentarily tornado disaster.

When Azlina saw the bloodshot eyes, she tried her best shot to comfort by holding Angela's hands up. Lucas came along. He was touching her head gently. She just burst everything that came into her mind.

She said 'I have been looking for you for all these years. I have been writing letters to you every single week with the hope that I might get a reply from you. I never thought we could meet each other just like that.'

She laughed and said, 'Look at you, you're so sweet. How could I ever not remember you? A simply lovely letter from you had reached at the first week when me and my family were busy preparing stuffs for the purpose of going abroad. It was substantially because of my elder brother ....'

'He was going to New Castle to further his study in medical field. I really wanted to tell, but it was all too rush. A plan to move temporarily to United Kingdom for a few years was proposed. As my parents' prior attention is always on my brother. You know it is always not easy to fit into the new environment that you are not familiar to, and the meanwhile my father wanted to start his business in United Kingdom. We then stepped on the cloud in the following weeks.'

She took a break as well as an extending breath as if she was too tired of talking continuously. She resumed and smiled, 'I really wished to reply your letter but I could not remember where to send. My dad could not let go of his car exporting business. So, I and my mother together with my brother who is now a postgraduate, hereby came back to Malaysia. You never knew......How much she misses everything in Malaysia so much, so do I.'

She showered Angela with her sweet smile. 'When we got back to our home in Johor Baharu, I only found a numberless unopened letters in my mail box. There was not enough space in the letter box to contain the letters anymore. The postman just left a note to us that there were still many letters in their office........'

She stopped talking for a second and reverted back, 'As I explained to my mother, she just could not believe what she heard. She never met someone like this. Who would know someone to continue writing letter to me?? A person she did not really know without getting a reply for years. I also never thought of this to come.'

'I thought you might forget about me after a few months or more. It is just so touching, so I begged her. Wah la ..... Here I am. I just moved recently. I read your letter before. Don't you remember what you mentioned in the letter, do you? You don't change much and my memory is not lost. Thus, it is just a piece of cake to find out ......'

Lucas was looking at both of them with his uninterrupted and unbroken concentration to listen. Someone came in abruptly by saying 'Three of you are still here. The door is going to be locked up. So, hurry up.' She got shocked again. They just turned around to see, 'It is Holly.' Lucas said.

She was only recalled that her schoolbag was still in the class. It could never be any better. Grandma was waiting for her at the entrance there. After hearing what she said, she just ran down the stair and packed everything on the desk up, Lucas and Azlina followed her back.

The three musketeers just walked out from the class. To walk down the hallway, she saw grandma wiping her face with her handkerchief off the tiny droplets of sweat. The despondent feeling was then filled with culpability.

Grandma blinked with her eyes closed, she just waved her hand at them. Angela told her apology. She just smiled and spoke in a friendly tone, 'It's okay, I do feel refreshing after sweating....' A giggle was heard.

Azlina went on and said, 'I agree with you grandma. It's undeniable! The scenery is the best memory! However, I really don't like if I don't sweat for a day. I just could not imagine how I went through the years in the snowy land.' She doubted, 'Really?' Grandma was looking clueless about the girl who talked to her. Angela went up and said, 'Let me introduce my new old friend, Azlina.'

Grandma said to her, 'Hello, Azlina. Nice to meet you. My daughter always said the same thing as you said.' Azlina said, 'Your daughter? Where is she living right now?' She and grandma was speechless for awhile, grandma did not know how to answer at all. The surrounding was getting unusually uncanny.

Nevertheless, she knows that the galled eyes can't run away from this forever. A voice was released without feeling disquieted, 'She is now in heaven together with my father.'

Angela kept on telling the complete story about how they met. Grandma was amazed like she just nodded her head funnily. Having heard of that, grandma just invited her and Lucas to their house. She noticed the on-going conversation like old friends for being strangers in years. Lucas and Azlina agreed. Grandma called their parents just to get the permission of delegating the responsibility as to their kids.

Not forgetting the weather today, when she looked up to the sky with the eyes closed. They then walked to their house under the skin scalding fire ball. The sweats from the bodies had made the clothes became transparent. However, it was never meant to spoil. The three musketeers even sung along the way. She feels lighter today. Is it because of loss of water in body or you have let go the ancient bulky stone?

While walking back home, the noise they made was the highlight of the street. People could not stop looking at them. All of a sudden, they became stars at daytime far from the solid ground. She knew the feeling would come haunting her again even if it was only last for awhile.

She got prepared for this burden. The noise had now stopped. Unexpectedly, there was a girl standing in front of the gate of the house. The legendary spooky house! Her back was against them. All they could see was her waist length black hair. Azlina asked, 'What's wrong?' When she heard people talking at her back, she tried to turn her head around.

To avoid embarrassment, Angela quickly tilted the followers to walk forward when she was about to see the real faces behind her back. It was something new about this anonymous neighbour in the colourful town......

A PLAN TO SURPRISE

<u>3/5/2001</u>

1 An usual date

The sky was perfectly clear in this morning today. You could barely see cloud in the sky. However, it was strange that she could not even see the sun that lightens up the mickle sky. It was in deep blue like the water in the ocean. Its visibility of virtual purity in aesthetic natural phenomena had frequently impressed her. Hopefully, it was not the last time for her to satisfy the eager for natural aesthetic beauty.

Besides that, the sounds they made attracted her attention as well. She spotted. There were three birds hovering in the sky. It is funny to say that they would stop flying and take a break by clinging on the lamp pose. The moment she saw the picture, the familiar image reflected in the brain. They were comparatively looking alike in certain mean though the sizes were never the same.

It was the break time. As usual, the three musketeers were sitting in line on the park bench after putting up flab on the tummy at the nearest canteen. Lucas was asking Angela the reason why she always stares at the sky, while two of them were chatting like she was invisible sitting in between them.

She then turned her head to Lucas. She looked at his bubbly chubby face. She was still as she wondered about the untold question that why his eyes always looked tearing.

She later turned her head to the right. Azlina, the girl next to you, is beautiful as she always is. What got her eyes frozen the most was her yellow daisy clip on her white hair scarf instead of her pretty face. She was wearing Baju Kurung with a white top and a blue long skirt.

It was really intriguing that the daisy clip had been so naturally outstanding whereas it had been encircled with white colour. It even made her looked more enchanting.

I guess this was why Michael always said he thought he was looking an angel, Azlina. So, he called it love at the first sight. I don't really believe in his nonviable postulation. Its reality sounded ridiculously unreliable. As I always think thing keeps changing, I just don't fall for the ecstatic susceptibility of the butterfly feeling. Let's me make myself clear, this is not the game you should get into.

She was caught laughing by her own again when thinking about this funny thing. They were just floating in the state of disarray. Suddenly, Azlina asked staggeringly, 'Hey guys.. erm… You know what?? My birthday is on the last second day of the month of May. My mom did not tell me where to celebrate this year….. She might have forgotten about my birthday.'

Angela jumped up from the bench and said, 'It is okay. She may be reminded in latter time!!!' Lucas then stood up and said, 'Yes she will!!' Azlina just grinned and the jig makers were hand in hand while walking back to their class separately after the bell rang.

2 This meeting is a dern

After the bell rang, she knew it was time to go back home. She was rushing to pack her school bag. It was because she did not want grandma to get burn out.

Before she walked out from the classroom, it was a habit to turn her head back to check out whether anything on the desk was left unpacked. That was a greatest advice ever applicable each time before leaving as well as a reminder in life.

She saw Lucas standing in front of her from the minute that she turned her head around. She was freaked out with a thunderous scream, 'Oh my!!! How could you scare me in this way!!! I could have died if a heart attack did pay me a visit!' Lucas smiled, 'I am so sorry.. Haha.. I thought of tapping your right shoulder but you already turned your head around.'

She grunted. Lucas heard a low and guttural voice, 'You will never change.' Angela then looked around and asked, 'Where is Azlina?? She did not follow you??' Lucas answered by way of being positively emotionally aroused, 'She went back to her house as her mom wanted her to as it is her parent's 10th year of marriage anniversary. They are going to celebrate in long distance. Isn't better for us, is it!!!??'

She was just staggered. She did not know what to say at this point of view. He went on to say, 'Come on. Don't give me that look. If she was around, we would not be able to make a plan to surprise her during her birthday party. Right??' She wondered, 'Surprise??' He just dragged her to walk forth and said, 'Your grandma is waiting for us downstairs.'

They just walked back home together with Lucas. She could actually feel people were looking at them for the reason that we all knew. Lucas looked a little bit different today. He seemed to be extraordinarily talkative today. I guess it just started ten minutes ago. She really wished there was a stop button to make him take a break from talking for awhile.

It was hilarious, and so there she was again. Lucas just ignored the strangely laughter and kept talking with grandma. Grandma's friendly invitation to come over. This was why she still saw him sitting right opposite where she was sitting on the dining table.

Grandma then served them Salmon steaks. Lucas said, 'I love it. Thanks grandma.' Grandma replied, 'I am glad that you like it. Enjoy it with your gay heart.' She just walked back into the kitchen. Angela quickly asked, 'Dear Lucas. Is it my turn to speak??' He answered with a wickedly cute smile, 'Of course, darling. Feel free to say.'

3 A plan to serve the best memorable gift

She asked, 'What is your plan to surprise her??' Lucas said, 'The plan is easy. It just revolves around something we both know. I am sure that we will rock and roll her birthday!!!' She tried to ask him repeatedly about his plan, as the action of planning was remained ambiguity. He insisted not to say until the day of tomorrow.

He should be able to tell the face of impatience in waiting and also how the heart of curiosity could drive her crazy. He still kept rejecting the humble and frank request. He just went back home after the empty dishes. He was so annoying to the extent that, he asked her to remember to remind of him about the plan in his mind.

She really felt frustrated about his nasty attitude. Whatever she did, she was thinking about this question for the whole day even when the wrong calculation was done. When she was on the bed, the night appeared to be energetic even the weather was sweetly comfortable for a good night sleep.

So, here she is showing the trace marks on the priceless diary, though she did not intend in the first place.

WISH YOU WERE HERE

30/5/2001

1 The cake is remained intact

Angela is in moodiness tonight due to the defeat of expectation. She started to recall back the moment that your eyes stared at the cake she and Lucas baked together. Lucas was with her until the sunset soon after they got back from school. Yes, only two of them.

It was not happened in the way her and Lucas were originally anticipated. She was not here to celebrate. Anyhow, she should never be blamed. It was just a twisted fate. As the told anticipation was turning crooked, she never mentioned anything about what had happened in the last few weeks. Angela also thought her big day would be an unadorned one this year, though it was her twelve years anniversary.

Despite the time of busy doing their science project, she pleaded grandma to entreat by teaching on how to bake cake. Frankly, she never cooked anything in the whole life. This was the very first time and also the very last time. Lucas was laughing at her suggestion when he first heard it.

He felt this idea was annihilable in the sense that it was unreliable. What a joke for a beginner to bake a reasonably edible cake. She really felt humiliated just because of what he said.

She refuted, 'I thought you said you got an idea but eventually there was nothing I could hear from you. Great! I would just follow what you said, if you had any other better idea. If not, please do me a favour, keep quiet and assist me in producing a birthday surprise.'

Again! He patted her right shoulder, smiled harmlessly and said, 'Alright. Since you are so determinative, I will assist you as what you wish for.' She just rolled her eyes and said, 'See, told you that you would not think of something better. Now you know…. At least I know Azlina is in fall love with cheesy like melting chocolate.'

They thereby decided to make a chocolate flavour surprise for her this year……

She went to their school library together with Lucas after school time last few weeks ago. Azlina did not notice about their unrevealed intention of the potential surprise. She told her to go home by herself. It was because of the need to submit the finished science project at Rehan's house with other group member, namely Michael.

Azlina found out Lucas would not be available as well. It was all too sudden. She just wondered why everybody got so busy recently upon guitar lessons and science project so suddenly. They did not tell lie to her. It was more like hiding the truth from her.

It was all derived from good intention. It meant no harm in the first place. Lucas did go to the guitar lessons after the search for a suitable recipe in the library whereas she went to Rehan's house to touch up the science project that they have been doing for two months.

2 The winter snow they are creating

Speaking about the science project, it was a wondrous job that three of them had made. Tracing back to two months ago, their science teacher had enunciated that all the students in the class had to be accomplishing for a presentative theme in science term. It is meant for the governmental examination in the final year of the primary school year.

She was distributed to join the battle crews. Rehan, my project buddy, is a cute Malay girl. She particularly likes to put up herself with girlish long dress. She definitely got her own sense of fashion. She was the one who suggested to work on diagnosing systematically about the seasonal winter weather as this was something she really wished to explore.

They both agreed harmonically. They intended to demonstrate the phenomena in an actual example. This is how it got started: 'They thereby used a large rectangular transparent plastic container as the base of illustrating. The best part would be that they even decorated the container like a normal uncultivated land, which had pond and field beside it.'

They then sealed the container properly in order to ensure that there was no escape of the evaporating water droplets in the environment of the container. After a few days, the pipes separately were inserted on the left and the right hand side of the container. The two rubber pipes were equally and significantly purposive.

The pipe on the right that was containing the cold air, which was derived from the ice box. On the other hand, the pipe on the left would transfer the scorching hot air, which was collected from the boiling water, to the container. They did make a few attempts in creating winter snow in the nameless land but failed. Millions of brain cells were sacrificed in the name of homicide just because of the defective snow converting system.

They were thinking the failure might be the reason of repeating the same method. It could be that the simultaneous transmission of the cold and hot air. So, they changed the tactic of converting. The pipe consisting hot air was first being activated.

The hot air was then being released and was let to be mixed with the warm air which originally existed in the container. The cold air was then released into the container on the next day. Amazingly, the infinitesimal result they saw had made up their wide – eyed gaze.

There was a demand of improvement on the process of this demonstration, especially on its appearance. As the first born subject was originally planned for a rough demonstrating idea, they still have to make a proper one, if it is for the examination purpose. I guess she was too busy about the science project until she forgot to pay attention on Azlina though a notice of her to have something to tell.

3 Miles away from where you were

Despite all the hectic schedules, two of them managed to get together and gather at her house to learn baking from her grandma. They even had a sketch of how the cake should look like. They had been trying to experiment for two weeks before they actually produce a flawless one.

She just thought of going to give the birthday girl a surprise by bringing the home-made cake to school happily today. The students in class were wondering what was actually contained in the striking red box. She just grinned and unrevealed that it was a top secret.

During the break time, she went to see Azlina in her class, but Lucas waved his hand at her. While she was holding the cake she baked delicately, she walked to him with the bad feeling. It did not seem like a good sign. Her heart was beating like riding a roller coaster. It was an intensive moment.

She went near to him and said, 'Hi, Lucas. Where is Azlina??' Lucas pouted and replied, 'Azlina did not come today.' The rain was immediately pouring heavily over the milky sky. She then asked, 'Why??' He answered with nothing at all. It was way too fragile. Their bubble hope was bursting tragically. Two of them were looking extremely despondent...

She went back to the class with a disappointed figure. She did think of distributing the cake to them when eye confessions were seen. However, she still did not want to give up her hope on finding. She told herself, 'She could just fall sick!!!!'

When grandma came here from home to pick her up at school, their disappointment was heard, and thus Angela begged her. As she thought grandma would bring them to Azlina's house. She really wanted to find out what was actually happening as she could not believe she just went off with no sign. Grandma just could not hold on of her sorrowful plead, she finally agreed.

Azlina is living in the apartment that her adoptive father owned in Pulau Tikus. The place I know quite well. Before they thought they could enter the building, a security guard blocked them. He looked stable and energetic at the same time in his antiquated uniform. He then said, 'I am so sorry. Three of you don't look familiar to me. May I know that do you live here? Or, someone you know who lives here??'

Angela answered impatiently, 'I am so sorry too. We do not live here. I wish to go to visit the one who lives in level four, Puan Noorhayatimah.'

He then replied with a more relaxing tone, 'Oh I see, don't you know that she went out for a trip with her daughter early this morning? What I heard from them was they are going to celebrate her daughter's birthday today by way of travelling to United Kingdom. They would come back on the day after a week, if I am not mistaken.'

She could not tell how was the broken heart sounded like whenever there was a flashback. She went back home with them. The two of them just sat on the couch in the living room at her house. They stayed silent while the pouted faces.....

DETECTIVE CAME TO RESCUE

6/8/2001

1 What a tedious morning

On the basis that, our governmental examination is getting nearer, our school authority has recently stressed on this issue in repetition on the regular school assembly every Monday. She was originally feeling blossomed in that place when she heard of Michael's call for lining up. She knew she would be able to skip a few morning classes lawfully as it would take more time than she ever expected.

You might think she loved slacking, but she was just too tired to accept the dissemination of knowledge. She even felt sleepy after the temporary excitement she had while queuing up and waiting to go for the assembly.

She wanted to write down worth memorable things in the history book before an invigorating sleep yesterday, but she guess the glassy eyes were not allowing her to do so. As they never really opened tightly after a lovely body-warming bath in the late night time.

She went to the butterfly farm yesterday together with the number 1, 2, and 3. It was a date for four of them. A dream to go exploring with the persons she loved. She never heard of this until today. It seemed to be a fascinating experience in this farm which filled with infinitesimally great lives in that place.

The butterfly farm was located at Teluk Bahang on this small island. It was farther than the heavenly disguised purgatory she loved to go. She almost fell asleep in the cab even though it was not comfortable for that purpose at all. It was quite a long journey and moreover, the traffic was not as smooth as the leader anticipated.

The children who sat at the back seat in the taxi. They were initially vigorously active in the cab. The noise they made by talking non-stop in the first place and playing simplified games that they learnt from Michael in school. It was because they were excited about the potentially mind – pleasing trip later. However, the time passed like how the cab was trapped in the traffic.

She knew she was not the only one who felt this way. The only adult among them who sat in the front passenger seat, was taking a momentary nap as she would get waken up by the violent honking sound where she would not.

Nonetheless, they still reached the most anticipated destination of the day slightly later than the expected time. The farm was absolutely a large maze that she had ever seen. It was laden with natural foundations, such as flora and fauna.

They were elderly but sturdy tall trees along the walk path. Besides that, she also saw various species of pint-sized plants which produced flowers to infinity. They were all underneath the shield from the big trees.

It was like the little had been protected securely at all time. There were many small cottages found in the park. One of the cottages was the place showing historical story the park had gone through. Bingo! She thereby found out about the fact that this Penang Butterfly Farm was four years older than her.

What had excited her most was that they were actually standing on presumably the first butterfly house in Tropical Region. Another cottage was reconnoitred by the troopers walking hand in hand. They actually got stunned by what they saw. They were the dried zombified specimens of the insecta all over the room. She even saw the biggest moth's sample in the world, hanging on the wall.

They still seemed glittering in her amazed eyes as she thought in the first glance. A mine bejewelled with colourful gems of creativity was observed. However, you could still hear 'Ouch! It's hurt.' A wish was made to touch them as if her hands had gone through the transparent glass that framed them up.

Grandma took out her newly bought camera with a fully unused film. She started taking picture in a throng. She felt they were the shining stars in the bright daytime. They later went to the park located at the outer part of the farm.

It was a well – preserved wildlife park while she could only see many insecta and numerous species of bird creeping on the visitors. It was like they were too shy to come out and see them, except for the certain butterflies. A special thing was felt yesterday like the butterflies were flying around her knee there. She guesses it was how they were welcomed into this wonderland.

The children she brought here were running around in the park but she was standing like a statue with glowing head. A notice was sensed of streaks of grey hair shining under the reasonably warm sunlight. It was due to the weather today, it was not as clear as this morning when they got out from their house.

She originally thought it was just a butterfly farm which played the role of being the major tourism attraction in Penang Island. She just found out that how wrong she was. It was something more than a beauteous vase. It is an internationally recognised science research center as well as a place for the sake of dissemination of science knowledge.

The farm is also acting as an initiative organisation of protecting the natural habitats for the flying population. Prevention is always better than cure for the case of the extinction of the rare species of those precious little things. The breeding work is also carried out in the farm. The officers there who bear the name preserving the endangered species.

It was a worth tiresome day as a result of what she saw and learnt. They were hanging out in the farm there for the whole day until the evening took over the happiness in the noon. A gaze on Gurney Plaza, the famous tourists' choice of shopping complex in Penang.

As they had consumed up all the reserved energy in their body, they thought they should pump up something they lost at a restaurant in the complex. Therefore, it was proud to send Lucas and Azlina to where they are bound.

2 The casualty?

She eventually came back to the time where she was standing today when someone hit her back and caused her almost to tumble. She then saw the floating ground. She squinted. She turned her head around and saw Bella standing at the back. When she looked into Bella's eyes, she was wriggling for a while before Bella actually came to her.

She kept apologizing about her carelessness. Angela said it was not really her fault for interrupting her day-dreaming session as it was her responsibility too. At this moment, she looked at something else behind her back instead of her pale but glowing skin. It was Lucy. As usual, she was telling two of her best friends, namely Nila and Fish, about her new branded silky jacket which her parents bought her from Paris this time.

She sounded exciting while the other two who were standing at their seats respectively and looking foiled and thwarted at the same time. They separately were Angie and Yen. Angie is the one who was sitting at the front, horizontally three rows away from her seat. A cute and shy girl in the eyes of mine.

She and Michael really look alike because of their round framed glasses and not to be forgotten, their chubby face. Although Michael's enchanted eyes were always on the owner of the daisy clip, their classmates always teased them to be a perfect match due to their couple faces.

Every time they did this, she would just keep quiet and keep her head down in order to accomplish her homework. Angela never participated to make the joke as she could feel the dislike feeling of what they did to her.

She was not trying to be rude but Angie always has the tissue – numbing expression. She never smiled, laughed, opened her mouth, rolled her eyeballs, or even had her eyebrows frowned. As a conclusion, she even has no micro facial expression at all. Angela did try to approach by saying hello to her sometimes, but she would always be ignored like as transparent as the air molecules.

However, Angie was not just frowning her eyebrows this time, she even pouted like the Donald duck we were used to love. So, she wondered what was wrong with her today. At the same time, Yen was staring at her unreachable bag without blinking her eyes as if there was something melancholy attractive to her.

Angela noticed the subtle nuance of her as to something she did not know. She is generally a cheerful and talkative girl. She will always decorate her beautiful figure with a joyful smile. She is a new student she just got to know for just half the year as she just got transferred from the primary school in other state.

She seemed dull today without her bright smile. While Angela's eye sights were still laying on the gloomy, Michael requested everyone to start walking to the hall and hence, the group of army started marching forth while five of them were still standing at their place. Angela then saw Michael walking toward them. She wished to find out what would happen next but she could not get herself out from the team.

3 The anonymity

The hall was full of dark spot. The air was more than just warm while Angela felt cold inside. She then found the increased hypoxia in the tissues of her body when she first stepped into the hall. She could hardly feel the air. They were ordered to sit on the chairs arranged nicely before they came.

She just waited patiently at her seat for all the students to gather in this hall of fame. As she saw the nicely famed pictures hung on the wall, it indicated how bright the students here were. The assembly was started.

The student representative spoke with her blaring voice. They later started singing their national anthem as well as the state anthem with pride. They, students stood with their unusual straight back and holding their hands still to show respect to their beloved land. She invited our school headmaster to deliver his speech.

After hearing the lusty principal started speaking alone, the peacefully venturesome journey begun with the attentive eyes shifting wobbly. She only noticed five of them sitting at the back row behind her. Lucy was whispering with her friends while Angie and Yen were sitting quietly beside them.

Nevertheless, Yen seemed extraordinarily unusual. She seemed uneasy today. Angela even spotted her cross-eyed on Lucy. She could tell a strong and fierce emotion derived from her eyes. It could be said the smell of hatred was scented surrounding her. The curiosity sounded like that what had actually incurred the anger of the evil in that place.

While she was trying her best to conceive of what was actually behind the unpleasantly mysterious fog, she heard someone beckoning, 'Angela … Angela ……' She scanned around the environment to check out whose voice. She saw Lucas waving his hand toward her. Sometimes, she wished to deny the fact that his lovely smile on the cute face really drowned her like the flood out of the melting snow in that place.

She just smiled and asked him to keep quiet otherwise; punishment would be the consequence for not being discipline enough while everybody was looking at the stage. They were listening his speech coming undone. I guess it was true. In the meanwhile, she secretly peeped on Yen again. She was now rubbing her hands roughly.

She thought her hands was unclean in the first place, but she later told by the intuitive sense that it was more than foul hands. The assembly was finally over. She did feel so disappointed when the words 'The end' hit her mind like a rain storm in the drought. They were requested to go back to their classes respectively.

She then followed the main stream to float back to the where they should be at. She really could not feel her feet touching the ground as a frivolously giddy mind was appreciated. The world was like spinning rapidly. She tried to grab something to hold clumsily before she actually fell on the ground.

She became partially conscious but she could still feel someone holding her right shoulder in order to support her from falling. She could not see that person's face clearly but she was pretty sure that it must be someone she knew. She saw memory in pieces passing by. It was numb. A new jet plane flew though the surrounding was dim.

4 It was in the dark

Suddenly, she heard someone calling her name. She could not see a thing as it was too dark. She said, 'Isn't the voice sounding familiar to me??' She struggled with great strength to open her eyes. It was like the sun in the snow. She still felt cold but she did not feel as sick as ten minutes ago when she saw his face.

Lucas asked, 'Are you okay??' She looked at his watery eyes as she thought he might be tearing in any minutes. She later looked up and saw the discipline principal and also the headmaster. They were asking whether she would want to go back home and rest. If this was the case, they would contact her grandma.

She mulled as she was lost to decide whether she should be going back and seeking for a medical assistance or staying here like she got something undone to be accomplished. She abruptly came in. It was the class teacher. She was gasping even if she was trying to say something. The headmaster said, 'Why does everyone gather in my office like we have a meeting here??'

She said with her conspicuous eyeball, 'Something worst happened in my class. The girls are fighting over a jacket!!' The discipline principal replied, 'What!! Please take me to the crime scene, Miss Choo.' Both of them rushed out as if they were consanguine twins.

They were then disappearing like the wind blow. Their originally energetic headmaster. He seemed to be anxious now since a few seconds ago. He then asked, 'Angela, how are you right now?? Do you still need us to call your grandma??' She replied speedily, 'I am a lot better right now. I can go back to class now.'

He reassured by repeatedly asking the same question, before he permitted her to go back to her class. Lucas insisted to accompany her to go back to her class, and he would only go back to his own class if she was alright for the next twenty minutes. Furthermore, he was interested on the real life story based play showing in her class.

Angela pushed his right hand away from her right shoulder with a reply that, 'You are so mean!' The headmaster ignored her loud groan, and went out from his office. They just followed. They were walking quickly up the stairs and heading to their classroom. On the way back, she could hear people screaming emphatically.

They sounded bickering aggressively. When they reached there, Lucy was shouting at Yen, 'You!!! Must be you!!! There would not be anyone else to do thing by what the jealousy told!!!' Yen uttered loudly, 'I did not!!! How many times I have to say?! I did not tear your jacket apart!! I was not the one!! Why?! Why you always have to ruin my perfect day?? Why??!'

There were some students and teachers standing in front of her classroom. Miss Choo tried to calm them down by making vain attempts to take them to the principal's office with the assistance of the discipline principal. The headmaster went out again. He might be going to call for extra assistance. Yen did just wriggle while Lucy just thrust the discipline principal to the door there. It was all involving violent discouragement.

Michael who was standing beside her and Lucas, started to elucidate, 'After we came back to our seats separately, she heard Lucy yelling at Yen with her thunderous and tremulous voice. She claimed that Yen had torn her jacket into pieces for the reason only she knew. Yen kept denying it. Lucy first started to slap Yen in her face. This is how the war begun.'

She asked while holding her chin delicately with the right hand, 'So, it must have happened right before we got into the class.' Michael replied, 'This is the same thing I have been thinking…. There are three potential suspects. Only me, Lucy and Nila were walking together to the hall. Yen who said she wanted to go back to the class to take her wallet left in her school bag. Secondly, Angie who was walking so slowly until I lost her on the way I got to the hall. Thirdly, Fish who said who wanted to go to the washroom.'

She thought she was dexterous to reply, 'Alright, but why Lucy kept pointing her finger on Yen??' Lucas interrupted, 'I know why …' Despite the noises created intentionally, Michael neglected Lucas and continued to say, 'It was because of the unknown history. I just found out two weeks ago. Lucy was verbally assaulting Yen. I did try to stop her at that moment but we all know Lucy was a rotted person.'

'So, the motive is very obvious in this case if Yen was the perpetrator….' She said feebly while the sleeping eyes landed on Angie. She just kept shaking her head like a machine whereas Fish looked uncomfortable and shaky. While the adults were busy with the fiery fire in the water, she came to Fish who was standing opposite the teacher's desk. Michael and Lucas then followed her footsteps.

Those uneasy eyes seemed anxious when she walked nearer to her. Angela said, 'Hello, Fish. Do you mind if you tell me where you were before heading to the hall?' Her facial appearance looked paralysed. She tried to tidy up her bangs with her left hand. A narrowly deep cut was noticed on the extremity of her first finger of her left hand.

The wound was still new, as she could see fresh blood clot on the wound. She therefore questioned her about when she got the cut and what the cause was. Angela guessed she did not even notice as to the cut she got. She seemed surprised and said nothing at all. However, she never knew that a wrongdoer always cannot run away from his conscience.

It was advertent for her to say, 'You know what?? I have found blood stains on the pieces of the wrangled cloth. It could be the best talking evidence as if I just told the discipline principal to find the perpetrator who has cut on his hand. It is better to speak a spade a spade before people find out. The punishment might be minimized too.'

She suddenly burst into tears and screamed as if nobody was around.

5 What a joke!

The room was in tranquil for that moment. The argument of frustration seemed to be ceased from spreading wild like an incurable disease. She cried pathetically, 'I am so…sor.. sorry, Yen!! It was me…… I lied….in bad faith to Michael that I… was going to the toilet. I went back to the classroom instead because I knew it was a precious chance for me to have my revenge done when no one else was around. Lucy! You don't know how much I hate you! I know you are rich and you can get anything you want!'

She bent down her knees slowly on the dusty floor, 'Due to that basis that, you never thought of putting yourself into other people's shoes while you spitted out the sharpening words. The knitted sweater my late mother made for me is obsolete and abundant. I told you before it was the last gift I ever received from her. Why did you ignore that over and over again by expressing your cynical criticisms as to it?? I am not a dead person. I hope you know that!!!!'

The headmaster came in at the right time and said, 'It is not right to have revenge on others violently even though they treat you badly. The pride you left over on the edge of the cliff. It is not a wisely civilised decision. You have to be responsible of what you have done, Fish. It will be the same for Lucy in respect of her reprehensible attitude. It is my job to redress the mistakes my students do.'

Under the shield of peaceful sound, she stood wobbly. I think she really fainted this time. When she opened her eyes again, she was laying in her own bed in the hospital. Grandma grinned. Her lower voice. She was sent to hospital by the discipline principal whereas her class teacher called the fretful heart personally to come to the hospital. She said she had caught a cold and she needed to rest sufficiently in good quality time.

Grandma thought she would feel boring and so she brought her diary book without her permission. She should not blame her for this angelic intention. She just smiled while looking at her timid face. She said, 'Sorry grandma. I caused you in the state of trepidation.' She shook her head and said, 'Don't be silly. There is nothing to say sorry about.'

In the purplish evening, Lucas and Azlina came to visit her together with their parents. There is something Lucas said that shocked her today. He called her, 'Sherlock Holmes....'

The joke of the day......

FIRE ALERT!

1 Don't

The village was resilient but people were too scared to walk out from their secured zone. However, there was only one girl walking around the muddy alley. When you looked at her properly, it was realised that it was the girl you already knew, namely Angela. She was wandering around. It did not seem like it was done on a purpose.

She later noticed someone had been tailing her. She started to get panic now. The breath had begun. All she could hear was heart-teasing sound. She wondered what was at her back. She did not dare to look back but she just walked faster. Due to the condition of trail, she could barely move quickly.

This was the moment she felt fearful the most. Worry was part of the picture. The unwanted still came to you. That's all she knows. Unfortunately, she fell down on the swampy ground. Her plain white dress was covered in mud. She knew she had to get up to stay miles away from the place she was at right now.

She struggled but tried hard for getting ready to run. Suddenly, a pair of giant boots landed in front of the shocking eyes. She thought of the god of death at this time. It was never a good symptom. The owner of these stained boots pulled her up. She looked up and saw the familiar.

She was literally screaming, 'NO!!! You stay away from me!!! YOU! BAD GUY! You better don't!' She closed her eyes to pray. When she opened her eyes again, an exhalation was released. It was blissful though she felt so unexpected.

She looked around. She then laughed by herself. It was because she was still on her cosy bed. I guess she was just swaying in the aftermath of the adventurous incident. After a shocking dream, she was sweating like in a shower. She could know the fact she could hardly sleep back. She rolled her yolk eyes.

At this time, something far on the desk had caught the zestful sight!

She rushed to get up from the bed. She might make people wondering what the spotlight to her was. She tilted the chair from her spaceless desk. She then sat on the chair clumsily. Her hands were on the diary book.

She thought to herself, 'I just know how to spend my sleepless night!'

2 I was the victim of yesterday

The flashback started to be shown. Time passes but not much changes. It was the beginning of the yesterday. It was a nation-wide celebrating happiness across the country. The time we all remembered how this all time summer land came to live. The effort from those in heaven had contributed. We never wanted to lose the gifted peace at all.

They finally had a valid reason to skip the obligation. It was nothing more than the delightful anticipation. The three musketeers had eventually gathered together ever since the last time in the first week of the month. She never wanted taking away the fragile smile from her snow white face especially yesterday.

Grandma was the tour guide again in this planned trip. She first brought us to the crowded parade. It was purported to incorporate the multicoloured elements of our people into the demonstration. It was so fun as she could now see the real motion instead of the pictures on the book.

The performance was stunning. That's what grandma told her from her quietude. By travelling with the familiar way, they needed not to worry about the traffic. Therefore, the journey was remained pleasant. The kids could talk whatever they missed out at school at the back seat.

The destination they now saw. Grandma told to have lunch before the window shopping. The moment she stepped into the mall, the amazed sight was on her? It was something she could never figure out. I guess it was because of the dress she wore that day. They walked up the escalator. It was way too slackening.

Azlina suddenly stopped her latest conversation and said, 'Are we going there, aren't we?' Grandma's eyes were telling Angela, 'Yes, of course darling! I just know it is our favourite restaurant ever.'

Angela knew what did it mean though she was speechless......

As they walked, she felt glad that they could actually enjoy a normal holiday without unexpected disturbance. However, the day did not really work as how it was planned. A deafening sound was heard abruptly. It was the activation of the fire alarm. Everybody was thinking about the seriousness.

She could feel the crowded place was tensed up. So, the security guard came at the right time. He instructed, 'People, stay calm and please follow my footsteps. I know where the safest place is.' People started to move swiftly. They kept pushing around from where she was originally standing at.

She eventually fell when she knocked on the steel dustbin. She was frozen for a while as she thought grandma would come to hold her up. She was waiting while people around passed her by like the morning traffic. Finally, she refused to continue the long wait. She looked up and realised she was alone in the horde.

She stood up forcefully but she felt the pain pricking over her right leg. She squatted down to look over. There was a lonely wound on the outer part of her calf. It was gradually bleeding. That was why she had been numb to notice this.

It was a really disappointing moment. She was left in the uncertainty. No trace was sensed of where they were. Her face started to get wet as she wondered where they could possibly be. A deep breath was intended for the strong faith. She got up and walked with an uncoordinated movement. She tried but people around did not seem to allow.

She was chased away from the mass to the corner. It was made to be impossible. She did not want to give up. She knew she got to get out of the building in order to see them again. She noticed another way out. It was right in front of the stiffened eyes. She knew this building very well.

She had been here for countless time. She thought she could make it. She bat her cold lips and decided to walk towards the confident plan. She was hopping instead of walking. It did take her some time. Finally, she was here at the door of surviving. She stopped before entering. She turned her head to look back.

3 A feigned scenario you never foresaw

Her hope was not becoming the reality. The throng was continuously walking in the contradicting direction. She was determined enough to walk forward. She pushed the doors but it was stuck. It could not open. She was anxious to think of what was happening. She never knew this to come.

Later on, she tried many ways to stay cool. Her eyes were scanning around. Suddenly, the light was finally not on the hook. She was now realising the door was meant to pull but not to push. The door of desperation had eventually opened. She quickly hopped in and grabbed the handrail of the stairway.

She walked down the staircase gently because of the newly wound though it was a frivolous action. She then saw the paint on the deliberately greyed wall. It was written there number two. She then thought, 'It was only the second floor!' However, something got her feeling freaky there when she heard people talking down the stairs.

She walked so softly as if she was the intruder to the private meeting down there. An intensifying, rough voice was heard. 'What we are going to do next?' The coolest reply was now saying, 'Don't you worry. We have our men to evacuate the exit! We just need to be patient now until the call for escape.'

Angela knew it was not something that she was supposed to listen. She started to get paranoid. She thought, 'Should I go back to the top or go down to investigate the flying speculation?' She just could not stop the thought of curiosity though she was not brave enough to do all the stuffs in her mind.

Without knowing the fact that she was stepping down the ladder, a cockroach was crawling over her feet. She was literally screaming out loud and jumping high from where she was. She slipped but she was lucky enough to react to the unwelcoming object. Her palms were on the icy handrail as she was trying to stand up.

While she was focusing, she still noticed an excessive pair of giant boot at the front sight. She was now sharing to look up. The owner of the boots said, 'Hey, little girl! I guess you should learn your lesson now! Better not to know too much about reality!' He pulled her up and dragged her to the group of strangers.

He spoke to them, 'I think she heard of what we said! How to settle this?' Her fear caused her substantially losing voice to speak. She saw those bulky black coloured bags on the floors. 'What are you looking at? You girl! You really have the courage to know this! I dare you!!' She saw the reflection of this sun glasses.

She was tongue-tied. She wanted to tell how painful she was to have the owner of the giant boots to hold her arm like that. She did not even have a chance to do so.

They ransacked their bags. She momentarily saw a collection of golden jewellery. Her frowned eyebrows and the dropping jaw attracted bad faith. 'I bet you must have wondered where those valuable jewellery came from! Right?' Angela was shaking her head. She would never want to answer the question of death.

However, it could not prevent him from talking. 'Isn't that obvious about what we are trying to do here?' She choked as she smelled the cigarette mouth. He continued blatantly, 'It is like drinking water to fool people. The fire evacuation was intended to be brought to the theatre. Once we are notified, it is the time to say goodbye to you, girl!!!'

4 The hope is in your hand

The dragon tattoo was swiftly moving while the hand proceeded to...... She thought, 'Oh my goodness! It is a fire gun!!' It was pointed at her sweating face. They were very impatient as they kept looking at the watch. The walkie-talkie was so soundless until she heard her sweat dripping off her face.

'Wait a minute! Someone is murmuring over the walkie-talkie!' The hairy chin was moving. 'Wait for confirmation then only proceed! Stay calm!' He looked at her with her reflection on the sun glasses. 'It's~~ It's safe now~~ Everybody is out!! Just stay right at where you are! We have called for help!'

She got shocked. She knew that she could not just wait for the dreadful moment to come. 'I... I... I personally think... it is better... to bring me with you guys. As... as... you all apprehend, criminals are the condemnation of people like us. It is never safe on the incriminating path. I could be your amulet.'

The pointed gun was shifted. 'She is right! This is just a double security.' Here he was again, 'Pretty smart! Alright! This is just for the sake of our interest. Remember! We have control here!'

She was too afraid to look straight to what is behind the sunglasses. She looked down to the unclean floor.

She knew it was not within the realm of possibility. She had to try. At this moment, Lucas was telling her that he would be the right-sided guardian whenever she needed him.

It was not genuine to hear these words. She knew. Lucas was not around. How could he potentially come over to save her?

They were whispering in front of her in group. Those sunglasses were looking at her again!! She was going backward. She thought it would be the best time to execute the escape plan. It was by no mean a successful thought. When she stepped on something, she turned her head backward. She heard, 'Nice try! Girl!' It was the owner of the giant boots.

He clung on her arm like she was the hunted rabbit in the bush. She disliked it but it was way too early to voice it out. She glared at him. He shooed with the evil grin. I guess the uncanny interaction between them had caught someone's attention. She saw her own reflection on the sunglasses again.

Every one seemed to respond to this authoritative command. They started to move as well as her, the volunteered hostage. They went down the stairs gently so that no one would notice the biggest risk they were taking. She just kept quiet to pick the right time. It was like you could hear the clock ticking.

Many hearts were pounding hardly. She disgusted as she never wanted to be part of them. Finally, they landed right in front of the door which was a step away from the heaven they thought. She thought, 'This pair of sunglasses must be the leader. How to make use of this advantage?' He sent the flying dragon to go beyond the door.

There she was again. She offered a crazy idea. She said confidently, 'Let me go with him! They… they… they might be more cautious to take preventive steps as I would be on the list of consideration. It… will… ease your escape plan. Seriously.……' He looked at Angela's sweaty face. She knew it was hard for him to trust as the hesitation caused the silence.

He uttered, 'Alright! Dragon boy! Make good use of her. Go out to inspect the surrounding. Report to me. Please make sure she is with you all the time!!' The said dragon boy dragged her out with the gun pointing at her. She thought, 'Here it's come!' She could sense the nervousness he had over her left arm. It was all wet.

The alley at the back was suspicious. There was nothing at all. Suddenly, someone shouted, 'Freeze!' It was a shocking word to hear at this moment. He was loosening her arm. She knew it was the best opportunity to run and hide. She flung his arm away and ran at her best speed with her eyes closed.

She fell again as she knocked a hurdle at her front. It was painful. She opened her again. It was the giant boots. She was scared to death. She kept screaming, 'NO!! PLEASE DON'T HURT ME!!!' A rigid voice was then heard, 'It's okay now, you can open your eyes to see those standing around you.'

It was the policeman! No joke! Later, she perceived those beloved eyes. She was too numb to feel the luck like this. The policeman came up and apologized. 'We are sorry, little girl!' 'Why? I thought I should say thank you for saving my life!' She wondered desperately.

'It was all because of the planned drama.' He tried to tell with sincerity. 'Planned? Do you mean it was intended to happen?' Her wide-eyed gaze seemed to scare him off. 'This is not something meant to be told. I am sorry, girl! People around the historical town are now safe!'

His back was reflecting the hero of our hearts......

TWELVE MEANS MORE THAN JUST ONE

<u>4/12/2001</u>

1 Work smart, perhaps play smart

Today is her twelve years old birthday. The military outfit I saw. Wearing a sailor tripe skirt with a hemline at the knee and a plain white shirt on top. Her claim of the fashion trend for this year. Not just that, it was because of her personal favourite too.

Many voices of opinion were heard, including Azlina as well. Masculine elements were shown with lesser feminine flare. Only she disagreed.

However, what people think is never an issue. As she really thinks it is meant to be. The reason is justifiable. Her desire on the stronger side to be in the show but not the weaker moment. She thinks, 'It's the time.' The silvery head should know by now that the little girl is not she was used to know anymore. The situation is now overturned. The capacity that she is keen to be shown but she does not know how.

As a result, I guess it is never easy to change others' perceived images on you. It does not matter now. As this is not the spotlight of the day. It was her birthday instead!!!! They all were celebrating the birthday of the rhapsode. At the same time, by bearing in mind about their graduation farewell, it was just like a 'two in one' flavoured milk.

So, an in house party was held. They were here so early. The moment she said, 'they' includes the whole familiar world.

It is just so fun. Talking about the amusement, they all were enjoying the delicious delight foods that grandma prepared for them. It was comprised of Western and Malaysian elements such as, the green cultivated coverage in the moor of spaghetti (it has always been her favourite), fried fish slices with specially made chilli sauce (the localised sauce of Sambai).

The scent was tempting even it had not been into your hungry mouth. It was like the storage of grilled bananas in sticky rice containing in the ship like banana leaf, spicy or not curry chicken pizza, the appetizer – pineapple salads, last but not least, vanilla durian flavoured ice-cream as the dessert. I am hungry to just mention about it.

The animals were really impressed by her fine quality cuisine. It is really a grateful improvement in her cooking skill by incorporating her creativity into delightful cuisine. As a foreigner, she does quite well in learning various recipes of cooking Malaysian foods within these eight years.

While enjoying the tasty meals, card games were suggested to be imported. It did last for hours and when they did not even want to stop playing it. Despite the fun they had with those trendy games, the fact of being a music lover was never forgotten.

Seriously, she would start jumping up and down and spinning around theatrically. As she was dreaming of a performing superstar. The moment she was raging on the stage and singing with all her heart whenever her favourite songs were played in the radio.

Grandma just knows who she really is. Initially, she intended to give the highlighted a surprise by playing her favourite song in the classically modern like radio. When she heard, 'Oh -- my pretty --pretty--boy- I need you--Oh---my---', she went crazy by letting go the cards from the slippery hands, running to the radio, and getting ready to sing along.

Azlina just came over to her. They just started the joyful dancing and singing until the majority of the faithful congregation joined in. It was like the black haired followers were up above the cloud and not remembering the hard times during exam times. Something funny had happened today. I guess our ecstatic laughter had annoyed the neighbours.

2 You are not the one she was used to be anymore?

They were coming to her house and demanding for keeping the waking voices down. An apology was about to be heard for not being considerate and creating nuisance. She saw the mysterious girl standing outside together with the unsatisfied crowd. She could barely identify the stranger's face. Her long black hair was covering almost half of her face.

The long sleeves dress looked like the girl's dress I saw the very last time in front of the 'once upon a time' house. Angela tried to disregard the vexation.

She just took the gut to apologize to them first and then invite them to the party because the more, the merrier. Not to mention the earlier disturbance. They just liked it. She doesn't know whether grandma realises or not, this might be the beginning of the changes.

She remembers the familiar psychiatrist. The mental health record was tracked. The doctor always acts professionally. As he was explaining to grandma about the issue encountered. He then made a conclusion. Angela was thought to be introvert on the ground that he medically discovered of her weird habits as to nervous disposition, difficulty to express herself as well as not being sufficiently social interactive.

An elucidation was told. An introvert is not the same as shyness but shyness may be one of the symptom of an introvert. According to his professional opinion, an introvert who will generally thinks it is a relish to ponder what has been found internally.

When he wants to be alone, he will have to be. The justification is thought to be simply a need to regain his energy from a herd of mammal. As he just needs to spend time with his own thoughts. Although he may have good interacting skills, staying in the state of clamour for any length of time will be an automatically trigger for a getaway.

By rewinding back to the revelation, she really thought everything has transformed back to normal, I guess?? It was all started from since she has met Azlina. The only moment she just loves being isolated is when a muse of writing is found. The silent mode is always on when the time comes.

Since the first move made to invite the neighbours with a big grin on the snowy healthily face, they just looked at her with their friendly smiles. They nodded before they started wishing her happy birthday. She said 'wow' to grandma, when she saw people kept coming in. However, first and foremost, they pretty much enjoyed the party, especially undeniably the foods grandma cooked

3 Love is in the air?

Today was really magically pleasant and delightful. It is something worth to be remembered in mind. It keeps playing like her favourite melody in the big head. Adults just consumed the meals though conversing with each other.

For them, children uh~~ uh!!!, something encouraging and hilarious happened. I feel so sorry to say this, but there is no room for scepticism.

Michael had done something today with his highly praised pride. As they all know that his vow on Azlina, he is absolutely serious about it. This is because Michael was telling everyone in the party, 'I wants to be her groom in order to prove the eternal love.' From the beginning of the year, even until now he never stopped, ~~~~ loving her?

His vain attempt to get closer to her by deliberately going to 6B and borrowing books from the students. What's an excuse? He tried to ask borrowing textbook from her once. He never felt enough so a quest for her as to the house phone number when the day of the book to return. There was how he got the number. However, it doesn't look like an effective one.

Azlina was like kept giggling every time the name of Michael was enunciated. She just found it so funny. She thought he was cute for doing all these things. It was so sweet that he took all the effort just to get to know more about her. However, a disclaimer presents.

Time may travel speedily but this sweet proposition had reminded her of her parents. Before she got into the place Angela was forced to stay, she was used to have a intact family. It was constituted of a loving mother and a comprehensive father. Her mother was a full time housewife whereas her father worked as a scientist and Azlina was their first child ever.

It happened in a distinctive era. She could not actually recall back the old days but she could always read back the diary. A sole item she was inheriting from her mother. It was all started from how her mother met her father. Her dad was actually working in YEX Syn Corporation. This is really reminding me of the work they did together for the science project.

His official position was a well –known team leader of a group of incredibly bright scientists. Her mother was a member among them before she got married. They were working together by years and eventually, they thought they were the perfect life partner for each other. Azlina always thought it was because of their passion in science and the well-understanding of each other's needs.

4 The diary speaks for itself

Her mother kept mentioning in the diary. How the guy made her felt like she was the most lucky person in the world. She always thought that she got married with a flawless man. Someone who had all the beautiful sides and morally strong characters. By virtue of no intention to meet him on the street, the secretive admirer saw him carrying stray's cats and dogs back to his friend's operated stray pets' shelter home.

She continued their love story where she could undoubtedly be satisfied about his strong sense towards responsibility. He would risk his own life just to ensure others' safety. He would also take extra caution or even extra miles effort to guarantee every experiments or tasks.

There was one time, they were putting the machinery compressor they invented on a test. Everybody was thinking to have their intention to be realised. As a result, the changes on temperature would have been foreseen in Malaysia. Unfortunately, an explosion occurred during the time of experimental state. The lab was on fire, as a team leader, he did not go and run to hide, just to ensure his own safety.

Instead, he instructed every staffs to stay calm. He suggested to use wet clothes to cover up their breathing device. The moment everybody thought the evacuation was a success, and no one realised that she was missing but him. He told her after the incident that he did not know what had caused him to be brave and when he noticed that she was still in the lab.

He just ran into the fire spreading lab in spite of the ominous consequences. When he found her fainted on the floor mat without any safety device on her, he just held her up in his muscular arms and ran to the exit and meanwhile, he was looking after the metal-melting environment, just to make sure there was no hurdle hitting on them.

Although she was not in the state of conscious, she could barely hear what he muttered, 'You are going be alright. I won't let anything to hurt you. It's my job to protect you!....!!.....'

When she opened her eyes, she realised that she was at the hospital. She thought by herself 'I survived.'

Surprisingly, she did not die out of the inhalation of the polluted air, which was full with the released molecules of the carbon monoxide by way of the chemical reaction of the acids mixture found in the lab.

She rewound back to what had actually happened and how she got into the turbulent state. It was hardly forgettable about the heart –thrilling, real-life based action scene. When she saw a nurse walking into the ward, an impatient question was heard. 'Excuse me, do you know about who sent me here and besides me, who else from YEX was also received medical treatment here?'

She was hoping for good news while waiting for the nurse to reply. The boiling temperature had driven her insane. The nurse just replied: 'Oh! There was a young good looking guy who saved you…. He……..' She just interrupted the nurse's speech. 'What happened to him? Please be honest to me!!'

Nurse resumed 'He… he got scalded on his back but the lucky of the unlucky. His condition is not severe. So, don't you worry. He would recover soon though the wound would be left as scar……..'

5 When dream turns into fallout

They got married because of the attraction of his strong – minded on moral value and also his sweet disposition. She was always reminded of cooking her meals even if he did not exactly know how. Unfortunately, they also engaged in divorce because of his strong moral value. It sounds a little bit of sarcastic, isn't it? The one is originally good for you, can end up being bad for you.

The culprit of their divorce was unexpectable. No more tolerance of his insistence on his passion of conducting researcher until the awful fact. He could go back home for only one time in a month. The level of pressure was not acceptable in her level.

She was handling everything trivial matters in the house and sometimes, taking care of Azlina by her own was driving her crazy. As a consequence, she was found with pernickety.

She just could not stand living alone without him in the life of marriage. He was not there for her when she needed him the most. By holding Azlina in, the blood shot eyes was spotted, Azlina said her mother was buried in the ground due to her incurable depression. He never noticed it. The reason as to any effort was never perceived to understand her.

Her mother died and his father went disappeared. No one knows where he goes. 'What past's past! I am happy with what I have now! I can feel sufficient love from my adopted family. I even got a big brother to protect me though I am not the real princess. Haha….. They even moved to Penang, just because they know what I wanted to….'

Angela would feel happy if she could meet the one. Someone who willingly takes care of her until the end of the journey. Speaking of this matter, it has never been easy, I guess. The precedents imprint the envisage. Hopefully, time will heal.

6 The right sided guardian

She thinks she just told herself that she just got something she never wanted to lose. Lucas who has been so nice to her from the first time she got to know him. He is so caring, loving, and polite to everyone he meets. He is also demure, intelligent, generous and kind-hearted person. Isn't he? She just could not believe that she could mention so much. The goodness about him.

However, sometimes she still thinks he is kind of weird. He always loves patting or tapping on her right shoulder when the big head is in front of the lovely eyes. This really scares her off every time he does. An ineffective quest to stop was heard.

He replied her that 'There is always a reason for everything to happen. The reason I always show up behind you is......' He seemed blushing with his head down. He fluttered his short spiky hair and resumed, 'iss....s.. I ..want ..to let you know that every time you got into trouble but no worries, as I got your back.' She doesn't know if it was a lame joke but when he said thing like this...... She could tell that he was serious with his words. It was because of his determined eyes.

Despite Azlina, Lucas has been the one she hangs out the most. The accompanied badminton classes, the numerous mathematic tuition class which conducted by his elder sister at his house, with Azlina. The fact of a well-known music lover. He knew and went for guitar teaching class to learn playing guitar. He just knows how to please a girl like her. Anyhow, the big head really appreciates it.

The beginning will always have an ending. The cheerful music still had to be stopped at certain time. Most of the fellow classmates had their parents to pick them up. The remained were still chatting in the living room but were surprised by an unpredictable voice. 'Azlina' A tall, moderate sized young boy showed up. I guess he is Azlina's big brother, a good looking young Chinese Muslim boy.

After she left, Lucas came to her. He seemed a little cramped but he said, 'I know the paper goose has meant something to you.... Upon your twelve years old birthday, I shall give you a bottle of lucky stars. They were all folded from the beginning of the year. I hope these lucky stars will mean something for you. Please remember..... Me and your lucky star. To shine and bring you out of the dark. I will stay as you want me to.'

She stared at his black watery eyes and smiled at him. He just said 'I saw myself in your big, round, brown – coloured eyes.' They just then laughed......

THE JOURNEY NEVER STOPPED
THOUGH SOMETHING IS MISSING

<u>4/6/2002</u>

1 She is gone again

The time passed by without you realising. Six months have gone as simple as that. She was quite busy throughout the earlier year. There still are four months to go. It will therefore be her first year in high school. Talking about high school, the very first at this place, the word 'fun' is meant to describe these experience. Obviously, she did not go being a lonely ranger. She has quite a lots of activity going on throughout the year.

The only regret is that Azlina is not here with her. They go to different high school because of the command of the sovereignty. She tried to find out the reason behind the decision but no truth was ever divulged. Angela could not even think of what to say when she looked at her melancholy.

The paper greetings are delivered. A hope to know how is everything going recently, perhaps the stories have been happening around her currently. However, it is just another disappointment. The only thing she could do is wait, and wait, just like last time. She is like addicted to the act of sighing.

Every time Azlina is remembered, the bitter seed is plucking the bloodstream in the body. She never thought of growing up would be the culprit of losing a good friend. It is really a despondency to know as to this unpleasant revelation. Nevertheless, giving up is never a part of their decrepit friendship. She still keeps the letter-writing habit as the part of her weekly routine. She therefore wonders why it has to be our destiny?

2 You finally know who you are

She never stopped writing to her since the very first week she got into this new place. The place by way of meeting new friends! Angela mingled with her new pool extremely well. She has been surrounded by laughter throughout the year. She has also been hanging out frequently with the new gang. They are Rehan, Esther as well as Joyce! The first gang coming to her life and which the one she fists conversing to.

Speaking about Rehan, she is the one Angela does feel familiar with. As the years they spent together in different space in the small city. She still does not know her well during the assigned period. She never got to know her in depth. During the time of walking backward, she was like falling in love with those two. She did not really wish to see anyone else when they were beside her.

Do you realise the small world you had been living in? Now, she hastened to redress. It should not have confined oneself even if you thought you already got the best. The world is awesomely kind, she should give chances fairly to widen what she was used to see. Hey, isn't that about 'Why just look at the small well while you live in a big world?', is it?

She might be choosy in impartation of yourself just because you think we do not share common characteristic, and thus it may not be ending with a happy ending. She will not run and hide from the mistake in the past this time. So, there should be a feeling of cherishing the beautiful things around her in future. Right now, there would not be anyone who does not recognise her white painted face.

Not to say, the popularity has increased. Just that she found that it was amusing in socialising with more people nowadays if to be compared with the past six years. She always thought the only grandma she had. She is still the one Angela needs for permanent but she will keep adding new people in the list of life.

Everyone of us knows life would not stop changing. It is never predictable for what is going to happen next. So, she just wants to live her life happily.

It is in the life of adolescence. It is about the members in her gang. An unusual love on making jokes on each other, and even teasing one and another. Nonetheless, madness is always absent by indulging ourselves into the state of anguish. I guess this is just the way they communicate with each other. Others may find it weird but it miraculously works.

I still remember that at one time, an innovative song writing and singing was held in the quarter of the year. She was jumping up and down, around the classroom. It was because of what she heard. Some students in the classroom were laughing at her. Question marks were trending. They thought she was funny for feeling excitement for no real reason.

Some students just gave her their turbulent looks because of her tumultuous reaction. It was like 'Okay, she is kind of cute but is she alright?' By thinking about this, she giggled. Rehan wondered and asked, 'What makes you so excited?' So, the question was answered as to the upcoming competition.

Joyce heard about it. Joyce just expressed her lovely mean words, 'Are you sure you are going to do this? Do you think you can?' She, suddenly did not know why but the unsupposed feeling of disappointment just crept in. Rehan saw her eye-frowning face. She just comforted her by patting her shoulder. She said 'If you love what you are doing, you should just go for it. We will support you.'

Esther and Joyce later put a smile on their face. What she felt abruptly was as nice as daisy, simply beautiful similarly as the secret guardian of the sunflower. They said, 'Yea. If you think can, you can; if you think you can't, you can't.' This jotting proverb keeps running around her brain.

She will always bear it in mind for the rest of the life as to her motivational quotes to keep her moving forward. She just wrote a song named 'Oh, Rehan!' for the purpose of the competition. She named the song as Rehan's name by reason of that she has been the muse contributed the most in her very first ever song writing experience. The hardship they all go through together in accomplishing their primary school's years, especially the uphill battle.

Seriously, there is no joke. She really loves writing. Particularly, when it involves music. She doesn't know why such feeling on what she is into. She just knows it is vital to the life of doom and gloom, she just feels what is appearing. Enormous effort is contributed as so far as they concerned.

On the day of the contest, her gang had been the obvious companions to the competition at school. They tried to cheer her up. I can still remember the feeling she had to stand alone on the stage with her shaky legs on that fearless day. Those fancy eyes were on this huge crowd she never seen before. When it was her turn, no.4, the fourth participant. They gave her thunderous applause, expected her to perform the song.

After they started to give her applause, the crowd followed. She just looked at them as she knew that they had a high expectation on her. She would not want to let them down, so a deep breath was taken in and ceased to proceed.

She then started to fulfil the loudest request she ever heard while playing the ukulele on her hands…..

'Oh, Rehan
You are my good friend
Oh, one of my good friends
I always love you.

We have gone through
The nightmare these four years
It's hard to imagine
How far we can go.

We have been feeling hard to survive under the upper hand
Struggling in the water, trying to reach the surface
We are holding on each other
When we fall apart
We are hoping our dreams come true
Yes, it will….

Oh, Rehan
I need to tell you this
The effort you put in
Will turn into gold

You gotta listen
I will always be with you
Though I may be worlds away
I will keep my words

This is our battle I know we're moving slowly
It always seems the journey has no end like munificent tragedy
But you will never be alone fighting against the dragon

Our dream
Is magical, though difficult
For all of us.

Oh Rehan
We know life fulls of thorns.
But we are getting stronger now.
Nothing will
Bring us down~~ oh oh oh oh~~'

3 Something that holds her up

It was too fragile to believe the reaction of the crowd. They were screaming like crazy after she finished the song. The applause she had was louder than the time before she started performing. This was extremely magical. As no anticipation was ever on the stunned mind. She could be performing perfectly well and people got to like it.

It was so absurd to the extent that she just thought it was all merely a dream at that time. The thing happened on that day which she thought risible the most was she won the competition. Funnily, she would be representing her high school for a song writing contest on the national level. This was totally unforgettable life changing experience. A new stage in life to build up her confidence with a rigid basis.

What a shock! She eventually got third prize among those amazingly incredible young song writers in the national level of the contest with the first song she wrote. This is also the unbelievable and adventurous story between her and her gang.

However, she could tell you how frustrating to hear that she had forgotten the old happily picture that she usually had back then. The old memory, especially the one who loves tapping her right shoulder and the promise he made that he always got her back when she was about to get into trouble….

A question is suggested for her tonight, 'Do you….or not? Is it real?'

LOVE IS EVERYTHING?

4/12/2002

1 Sad lonely day

Fourth of December is Angela's birthday, though it does not match the fact. However, today is a miserably pathetic day. She is now sitting alone on the bench at road side. She is currently a few hundred thousand kilometres far away from her house where it is actually located. It is an unusually tranquil night. As there is no car or even pedestrian passing by, but she can still see a crow hovering in the dark and then resting on the street light like it is homeless too.

The sound it makes. What a damage to the peace of the night, which she originally wanted to have. It is because it sounds loud and harsh at the same time. She took a long way bus to get herself here. By reason of that she really does not feel like sharing. Neither talking to anyone nor going back home to grandma. She wishes she never found out about that intriguingly horrific fact.

It is mind-storming. She really cannot take it. She knows what she is doing right now is bad. It hurts the person who really loves you. Grandma must be worrying about her by now as she still has not gone back home this late. She doesn't know why the delinquency occurred this way. The rebellious devil started ruling. The more you were told to do, the more…… You should know me better by now. She does not care what will happen next. All she knows is the wish to be alone in the middle of the night.

A peace of mind is summoned to think. Contradiction makes you want to hide the most. She wonders how to convince yourself to accept the truth even if you don't want to. In accordance with her wish, this is the very first time that grandma is not right beside her. It is hard to find someone around unlike the usual celebration of her birthday. The very least the two years old little booklet is a compatible companion here.

The world is getting way too complicated for her now. She holds it with her right hand and write. As words may describe better than speech. The one and only thing she could do now on the inky street ----------- writing.

'Everything
The night with nothing
I am here to mourn
Cry with voice trebling
To forget this thoughtful thorn.

He enunciated he loves me
But she forbids it to grow
He finally changes the theme
Of tomorrow story in his show.

Everything, everything
Is coronary ravaging
Anything of everything
Nothing is surviving.

I am suffocating
They are not able to help
She is intoxicating
Under her opaque scalp.

In the hallucinogenic state
I got nowhere to go
On this maze to stake
The pictures I do not forego.

Everything, everything
Is coronary ravaging
The past I think
None of it is surviving.'

2 It seems like it was happened yesterday

The memory just keeps coming back. She just sits here and thinks of the time when he said he would always got your back whenever you needed help; the time they kept in touch with each other just to find out how they were; in spite of the request by fate to diversify; their first time on the slippery pavement; the first place where the seed of love was cultivated, and the most unforgettable one is, the time when his very first confession he ever made.

She can never forget the sincerity she felt in the back of her mind by just looking into his eyes when the promise was convinced. She really took it seriously with all her heart. She guesses she is wrong this time. Not everyone never expected this to come, before she actually made up her mind to be with the destiny she thought, she was mulling in the state of trepidation.

Grandma was used to tell her that she can have the best companions which she thinks they are despite gender during her adolescent mind, but she should never forget her words. 'Remember to stay innocent and focus fundamentally on the educational basis.' She was advised for her future. True love will be put on test on congealed muck. The one who stays in the end of the journey is the genuine one.

By having that in mind, this is the reason why she hesitated for quite some times, to avoid multifarious ominous consequences. However, she just could not resist any longer when…….

The high school she currently studies is quite considerably far from where she stays. Grandma just cannot walk her to the school as she usually did. So, she will go to the school with school bus during weekdays. Nevertheless, she will still accompany. A long walk with her to the nearest bus station and waiting for the school bus to come. She will only leave if she confirms that Angela is going into the place which is planned.

She rarely goes straight back home after school because of the school activities. She has actively been involving in. Due to her trumping interest in music, she started to go for music lessons almost four times in a week. Unlike nowadays, she only learnt ukulele and piano during her childhood.

Her great impression towards guitar was observed from the time she participated in a music making national contest onwards. The thinking inspiration as a result of witnessing multitalented music students who are able to play various types of music instruments. She doesn't know why. Her love towards guitar is never getting rusty. It doesn't seem to have a reason to like it in the first place as you just feel your existence when it caught her eyes for the very first time.

Therefore, the way to go for tuition is always lonely. The tuition centre she goes is one – way tuition classes by reason of its strategic location and then it becomes a habit. Hence, it is really convenient for people like her. Many of the students wish to have transport or even a driving licence. To conclude the dreams, meeting at the same place will never be a norm.

For her, she goes there for the subjects she studies in high school as well as the most anticipated classes. It is because of the avoidance to cause any troublesome consequence to her grandma, and moreover, the tutors they have something. They are nothing more than just excellence, especially the guitar tutor.

He is so musically talented in the sense that he can just play his guitar with his eyes closed. That always makes her speechless. She really hopes she could be someone like him one day. So, public common bus has always been useful at this point. By virtue of its location, which is on the right side at the thoroughfare with the roundabout near her school, it has been a spotlight in town.

3 Something more than just friend

She met Lucas in the tuition class one day after she told him about this personally in the letter she wrote to him. Lucas is one of her classmates in the primary school that they still keep in touch with. Since then, he waited for her to go for tuition at school everyday from the beginning of the year. They even went to guitar lessons. Everything seemed like perfectly together as soon as he found out about where she had been going.

Despite that, one day, when they met up at the usual place. Enunciation was heard that day was something special until he wished to tell something. Angela got lost in his words. When a clarification was requested, he mysteriously denied to answer. He held her hand and walked forth from where she stood which she was pulled.

She attempted to reject his request and tried to get rid from his hand. On the basis that, she did not want to be a truant which was badly influenced by the companion as told by grandma. He begged her for a compliance with what he said. The feeling of pain was creeping in. She did not know how to differentiate that was it a feeling of sympathy or a feeling of appreciation towards our friendship.

She was struggling as to the conflicts that she had at that time; whether should you be absent to the tuition class as a result of following him to the place he wished to go; or whether you should just go with him. Regret is no more affordable as how she lost contact with Azlina. She really did not want to lose another good friend of her. She never knew the presence of Azlina in the party grandma held in the house was the last time.

As a consequence of internal vexatious disturbance, she still made up her mind to go with him. He brought her to a restaurant. While they walked into the restaurant, there was a tall, young man who dressed up tidily and he said 'You are here…... Earlier than the usual time, I heard from you on the phone. You said you will, right?'

She was led by the speed of light. She was looking at these two guys and literally knowing nothing. He told her that it had been so fun as a part time singer here. This longue bar was priorly based on the theme of country music. The environment was classical and warm. He first pulled the wooden chair for her and then only asked her to sit on it which very close to the stage he was about to get on.

He went on the stage to stand right in front of the microphone and got his bass wood guitar. There was something like a name carved at the front of the guitar which was somewhere near the bridge. She observed rigorously, 'It is my name on it!!'.

He started to deliver his speech before he performed. The attention was paid off. The song he wrote personally was dedicated to someone special by pointing his finger at her. It was a surprising prostration at this moment. She did not know how to respond but just stunned and listened to what he sung.

After he finished working, he walked her to the bus station. Along the way, he said that working here was an experience for like a few months back by singing songs of others but today was the first night to perform the song he wrote. He said it was because of her. He went on to tell, he was lucky enough to have his song to be performed perfectly in front of the beloved.

The thoroughfare was busy as how it was at the decent nights. While they were walking through the pedestrian's path, there was a car coming towards their direction. He noticed something went wrong and he just held her in his arms and his back faced towards the uncontrolling car.

The car swerved and hit the lamp post. Suddenly, the scene became blurry. It turned cold. However, no one got hurt as a result of this incident including the intoxicated driver himself.

She was emotionally touched by this intention. He could really put her personal safety as the first choice where their lives were at stake. She thought he could be someone who was genuine, honest to her, and in other words, he could be somebody she would be able to rely on. He never asked for anything more than she could ever give in. From that moment, she just thought she had found the right one.

4 Fate that brings us together, separates us

Grandma strictly opposed to their unity after the truth floats. She could not even concede for her decision any longer. She said she was too young to know what love is. She was so scared that her innocence would be ruined by her delirium state as to what he did for her.

In consequences, she had been neglecting her studies because of him as this is what she thought about her granddaughter. She never really understood her thought from her aspect. Due to this reason, she was grounded since then.

She was prohibited to go anywhere after school activities and except going to school. Grandma would go to her school and wait for her to come out. She would just warn Lucas to stay away from her as if they could never work out. Grandma just changed to another person which she did not feel familiar. It was all too fast. She lost her balance on the way.

She was so frustrated because of how grandma punished without even questioning. She stopped her from going to the guitar lessons and not even permitted her to go out with other friends of her in school during the school holidays. Angela tried to think from her side but she never did. It really hurts.

She just doesn't get it. How can grandma just do something to hurt her like this while she still thinks it is beneficial for her. So, Angela called him today and tried to ask him for help. She hoped. The disappeared Romeo would come. The unreasonable imprisonment that should be ended long time ago when grandma was out today evening. She wanted to buy something, which she did not mention comprehensively and Angela was left alone in the house.

It was a long lost relationship since he heard of the strong objection from grandma. The phone was picked up. She heard 'Hello?' It was a girl's voice!! She was so angry about this. She just hanged off the phone and went all over the house to search for the spare keys of the padlocks of the gate and took some money from her purse.

She went to her room and grabbed the diary before that. It was not plausible but she wanted the diary to be with her so much, she did not even think about it before she took it out. She then went out to the gate and unlocked the chain. She just started running after she had locked up the gate. It was unusual but necessary.

Here she is. Sitting alone on this bench in the drizzling rain during this time. She is also thinking about if. If it could snow right about now at the same time. This is because it fits how you feel right now. Nevertheless, she decided to wander alone on the street quietly.............

AN ACCIDENT THAT CHANGES OUR LIFE

<u>20/3/2003</u>

1 It's like waking up from a long night sleep

Surprisingly unconceivable!!!!! I could not believe what I saw today.

When I first opened up my eyes, the slimmest bright light that slanted through the window. It caused me to see things in black. My head was in great terribly pain. I could not remember what was happened yesterday. My mind was blank, like a piece of plain paper. Nothing was ever written on these unused papers.

This was outlandish. I could feel the space was spinning around. It was like no gravity could hold me down. After I gained full conscious, I tried to get up from the bed with all the strength I had. However, I found it bothersome. I only realised I was not lying on the bed at the room that I could barely remember.

I thereby wondered where I was. This is not a place I am familiar with. The wall is painted white but blue on the centre. It is like the blue thick line separated the room into two. It is a reasonably large with only one bed. There was not much furniture found in my room but only one rectangular shaped sofa.

It is a three seats leather sofa in dark brown colour. It is really outstanding in this room. The fact that I could only find the one and only thing here in this room which was not white in colour.

I tried to get down from the bed. I felt a sting on my hand. The exhausted eyes were shocked. I only noticed the medical devices which looked like a heartbeat detector beside the bed, which was on my left, whereas a long narrow tube connected to a hanged packet of transparent liquid which its head inserted to my vein on the right bony skin.

Due to the ground that, I could still feel the massive headache going on here, and thus, the right hand was moved speedily to approach the heavy head to support it. I then realised the big head was wrapped up with bandage. 'Is this hospital?' I was thinking to myself, 'What happened?? How do I get here?? Argh!!' While I started thinking about this roughly, a massive headache was incurred.

2 A stranger I met before?

A female nurse then walked in, 'Oh! You're awake. What a miracle!! I go to call doctor to see this!!!' She said tingly. After that she just ran out from the ward, a doctor later came into the apathetic ward. I could not recall where. I saw his face in my inexperienced mind but he looked familiar to me.

I was pretty sure I met him before but his identity was vague in the empty mind. Perhaps, he might be just a stranger I met on the street which I thought we were friends before and after. By thinking hard again, I felt headache that caused me in having trouble to speak with my brain.

My staring eyes. This doctor looked fashionable. He just looked like a charming physician in a movie. He fitted what he wore. A plain light blue collar shirt with white stripes on it and a dark brown cargo trousers. The most intriguing part was about his hair. He got an extremely shorn military style that split down the middle on its merit.

Furthermore, he would get the credit for his five feet ten height. I would say, 'What an enchanting figure!' For that moment, I was thinking about his girlfriend or his future wife. I seriously think this is hilarious. I just can't believe that I would have something like this in my mind while there was something else at stake. I really did not think he was who he was. He looked more like an unknown superstar to me. So, I muttered, 'he is stunning.'

He seemed a little surprised to hear what I whispered. Finally, he spoke to make enquiry. I just denied what I said. 'He was in silence for some time because of doubting my answer?' I wondered. He then went on to question me on whether I know what was going on. I just looked at him with blurry mind and said nothing at all.

The matter was still revolving about who the doctor actually was, and in the meanwhile, the connectivity of the question asked was analyzed.

I guess he thought I looked clueless. He continued his words to explain. The merciless story begun when I was knocked down by a speeding lorry approximately three months back. There was no wound to be found on the surface of my body but only nose-bleeding and bloodshot eyes during the time I was sent to hospital. It was medically rare. All the medical experts suspected that it was an internal brain hemorrhage. Most of them disageed to conduct a risky operation except for him.

3 I guess I was lucky?

The surgery was totally out of his mind. There was nothing within the general expectation, but he still conducted the surgery wittingly. On the basis that, it involved risk- undertaking as well as responsibility towards the family of the victim in the professional eyes of those medical officers. The ominous consequences that he did not want to realise, motivated him to take extra caution in performing this surgery.

Like he said, this was really miraculous. Obviously, I did not die out of the severe head injury. The speed of the recovery is absolutely amazing as he never seen anything like that so far as was told by the experience he had for these proper years.

'Argh!' The headache attacked me again. I saw pictures scattering in my mind. It was all in incomplete pieces. Before I got hit by a lorry, I was actually wandering at roadside; trying to cross the road but………

He laid his sympathy on me delicately, as I could see the light shining through the girlie eyes. He said I was the lucky one among those unlucky. It was a hit and run case. No one had found the driver as well as the lorry because there was no eye-witness in the event of the accident. I was only found and sent to hospital after an uncertified time by a taxi driver. He then stopped talking.

He provided me a medical examination by checking my eye sight, limb movement and asking question about my ability of remembering. After finished checking, he went out without anything said further. However, the nurse who followed him to walk out from the ward, turned back like she forgot something to do.

4 The diary of mine??

She went up to me and said with a jolly tune. 'Oh! Yea! I remembered that the time you were sent to hospital. You clung to this book so tightly. I guess it must mean the world to you! I hereby kept it in the drawer of the desk beside you bed.' She turned her back towards me and was about to walk out from the room.

Suddenly, she turned back again. She really got me nervous shock this time. She said to me, 'Oh! I forgot one more thing. If you feel cold, just let me know. I will turn the air warmer into higher temperature.' I did not really listen to what she said about air warmer as I was too curious as to the book she mentioned, so I quickly opened up the drawer on the right hand side of my bed.

I took out the mysterious book from the drawer. The cover of the book was definitely reminding me of something but I just cannot seem to have a certain answer now. 'Ouch!' I guess it never wanted me to think hard. I was suffering for the pain in the lingering afternoon before I could actually take my medicine and have a quality rest.

Notwithstanding what the headache did to me, I sat on the bed for the entire evening. It happened for me to read the so called my book in order to figure out the questions I have in my brain. Here is another disappointment. This is a diary book but there was nothing I could remember happening about what have been written there. During this turbulent time, I just let out my breath in a lengthy exhalation.

5 It's really happening

'Meal time!' A dedicately rough voice I heard. The sleeping eyes were opened. A fertile lady in apple green suit standing in front of me. She left the food on the bed table. The smiling eyes stopped at me. I struggled to look back. She said nothing then left the ward.

She later turned back. She eventually voiced out what she wanted to say. It was relieving. 'The sky colour is getting faded. It should be fine to live without the curtain.' After her words, she went near the curtain then pulled them out from the obstruction. The room momentarily became lightened.

I then looked out of the window. I saw white!! Nothing but white!! It was all in white!! Everything was covered in white. Gentle eye rubbing was never helpful. However, its sophistication was so beautiful. I was overwhelmed at this moment. Those pedestrians who walked on the street, were wearing thick coats whereas the snow was falling all over them.

They looked exactly like a living snowman. No wonder! Now I remembered why the nurse said something about the air warmer. I think most probably this is the reason why the air warmer machine was installed in the hospital. It might help to keep these people warm here in the aging building. What was trendy has now reached the other side of down.

Nevertheless, by reading what have been recorded here, it seems to be so contrary. Penang in Malaysia is a small island that this girl should have known it well for the period of fifteen years. I should be familiar with this place, shouldn't I? It is a tropical country which will mostly only have sunny humid days. It will never, and should never snow in Malaysia as identified in this historic book.......

The nurse went into the ward again and asked me to take prescribed medicine. I wished to ask her about this outrageous phenomena but I could not make it. She was too busy to stay still for even only one minute. I guess.... I shall ask them tomorrow....

This might be the thing to cause me lose my sleep at this time. I do not own any watch or any time indicator in this empty room. So, I will not know what is the right time to do the right thing. However, I guess I can tell from the dark cloudy sky. The weather is still cold as people are still wearing thick coats or jackets to keep them warm in spite of the fact that it stopped snowing a few hours back.

The snow that falls on the ground is not melting. The refreshing ventilation was my favourite. By looking out the window in the room, it just make me feel like I am watching over an animated picture and the window pane is just like the picture frame. In this picture, white colour forms the major parts in the picture as well as the 'frame'.

The following observation was that a yellow leave was whirling in the windy night before falling on the ground. What caught my revitalised eyes is the bright, round moon like a giant spotlight lighting up the white street in the dark.

It is all beautifully prepossessing as this is the scenery I never saw it before. I guess I am right as told by the book. The first ever white night I have been going through..... The night I will never forget this. All I know is this really pleases the sense of mine aesthetically.

If it does not snow in tropical country, there must be something changing the weather here. Hence, I wonder would it be the same in other tropical countries in any part of this world. Anyhow, I just got a feeling that something might have gone wrong in this beautiful night. As the weather is changing.., so do I ....

I don't know whether it is offensive to the real owner if it is found out that this much of words were written on the private book. I just keep on doing..... to spend my sleepless time.

WHO AM I?

1 It does not change

When I opened those heavy eyes this morning, I only realised my body was shivering without my knowledge. I just felt lazy to get up from my bed but the longer I lay on the bed, the more I felt the cold invading the senile body. I know why. I am wearing a hospital gown. It is all vacuum.

From what I observed, the fabric of the gown is composed of cotton material. These materials can only possibly withstand repeating laundering in hot water. Additionally, the funny fact is that you can only fasten or untie the dress with twill tape ties if your hands are reachable to your back..

Therefore, this gown I am currently wearing is obviously not a disposable one. Yes! It is cosy but not helping to fight coldness. Nobody is going to tell me this; nonetheless, I just know the salient utility always comes first. I guess I still have to wear it until the day I am discharged. However, I really could not stand the frosty weather like anybody else? As I knew it could make me fall sick in any minute.

Rolling over the freezing bed would make me lose chances to fall asleep again. My left hand was ready to enforce the command to help, because I still felt weak. Stumbling would be the drama of the day as if I got up from the bed. It was difficult but I tried. I wished to use both hands. If this became real, the needle would be penetrating the thin wall in the diluted vein.

So, I decided to let the constraint remained curbed. The drawer desk was trying to escape before I could open it. I eventually succeeded by stopping it with my feet. It was an embarrassing scene but the drawers were left wide opened. My utmost intention was to search for a jacket or anything that could make me devoid frosty bite.

No clothes were ever found and not even a single personal belonging in those choking drawers except for that book.

I was then thwarted and just turned my head to the window. That's how I spent my night with the wondered eyes.

Nothing was changed. All had remained the same as I first saw though the sky was azure with no thick cloud around ……

2 The second night

Limitation is part of the activity for the life here. Thus, the same thing I have been doing again and again. While I am sitting on the bed and writing on the anonymous book, I look out of the same window and still see what I saw today.

I can tell the snow is getting heavier. I can still feel the cold air inside a room even if the air warmer has been switched to a higher power. It is just so cold. I would not know how to survive outside this safe and sound boundary with only this funny gown.

The doctor came to see me again today. The moment I saw him, the feeling knocked me down again. I really felt there was something pulling us together. I could not hold myself any longer, and he finally heard my sheepish voice: 'Have we met before? Doctor, you looked so familiar to me. It was like I knew you in the older days before I got revolved around this turbulent space.'

I did not why I did, but still I did it anyway. He smiled at me while checking bewildered pulse and examining the printed body check report all at the same time. He is really a superman. It amazed me for sure. I wish I could be like him for a reason. This life brought me an indolent mind. Those doors are still half-closed.

He then replied me, 'You were just be reminded of something about your past, weren't you?' Having heard of what he said, I tried to think hard as to my previous life before the accident. 'Argh!' The headache just hit me again. However, a speculation came across my empty mind: 'He knew who I am?'. I almost fell from the heaped bed as I struggled. My hands held before it happened.

It was just a fallback situation. He stopped what he was doing and looked up. He then asked if I was okay. I told him my issue. He explicitly demonstrated the head injury of mine now. He continued saying it is normal for me to forget my past because of the malfunction of part of my brain as it has not yet fully recovered.

Due to the accident, I had undergone an unknown medical operation to remove blood clot inside my head. The medical experts addressed it as internal brain hemorrhage. He added on to say: 'When you were sent to me, you were in a critical condition. The internal bleeding in your brain was a life-threatening one.'

I was shocked for that moment and he paused. I could never imagine I was nearly pulled to the gate of purgatory.

'There was no surgeon willing to take the risk to operate, including me, someone who has just one year experience regarding this specific medical area. A little flaw could take you away without goodbye. It is something unlike I generally learnt. I totally had no confidence to carry out the surgery but my heart was with you......... Even if the operation was either a failure or successful, you might still be encountering the issue of permanent coma. However, you family convinced me to do this.'

3 Family that I don't feel familiar with

'Family?' I asked with the hope. I wondered that whether I could know more about myself. By recalling back what I read yesterday, I asked: 'It was a white lady with old young body, wasn't it?' He answered: 'Yes, it was. She said … As she said she is the only one you got and she is not afford to lose that much, more than you ever thought, but she would still want to take a risk and wish for miracle to happen.'

He stopped for awhile and looked at me with the eyes of compassion. I could actually feel it. He then continued to say, 'Miracle does not happen sometimes even if you wish for. I know how desperate she was as she did not want to give up on you by watching you leaving and she could do nothing else to save you. So,...... hey, look at you, now I know miracle does exist.'

He now grinned with a bright smile which would make you melt under the icy sun, 'You are really amazing! The recovery speed on your head is truly surprising!'. I lost my patient. I interrupted and said, 'So, do you know where is she right now?? Doctor, can you please tell me that??'

'She was used to come here everyday to do anything she could for the cursed sleepy head but I noticed that the effort seemed to stop one week ago.'

He finished saying what I wished and he thought I needed to know and then he just walked out from the room like he saw a ghost here.

4 Confined space restricts my mobility

Unresolved mystery keeps happening. First, the mythical weather changes and now the disappearance of the said family member. The pain on my head drenched me again…..

It was 4 p.m., I asked the nurse who is in-charged of my ward a favour, so that she could walk me to the park. As I still could not walk by myself due to the unwanted weakness. I felt feeble. It was probably because I did not really consume any food for the past three months but wholly depended on the glucose packet. The nurse had removed the supply now.

Recalling back, I don't wish to go under the needle again. I started to eat rice yesterday. The first potation was light and it never changed. I guess my appetite is the only reason they know.

However, I still wished to go out from my room I am currently staying. Based on the basis that I was so mystified by the things happening now. Moreover, I needed fresh air for a piece of mind. Despite that, she refused to do so. She thought it was treacherous for me to go beyond these walls.

She elucidated that it was just a newly beginning for you and the weather would be getting colder in time, especially when the night nearly came. She would not want to risk my life by taking me out. An abruptly weather transforming will incur the possibility of viral affection. On the ground that, it is going to undermine the sided condition of those armies to fight.

I did not really think she got all my trust on what she told, as I thought it sounded exaggerating. Anyway, I requested her to clear the doubt I had since yesterday.

As I asked her, 'Why it is snowing here, in Malaysia? To be exact, a tropical country??' By hearing what I asked, she was first trying hard to hold herself from laughing but failed.

5 Three months ago

She then said with a smirk on her coloured face, 'Lucky or not! Neither I know, nor anyone else. This is the trendy question that, not only we, Malaysian are wondering, the whole world is also concerning as to this hot topic.'

'On the face of the early investigation, it seems more like an artificial phenomena because all I know is Malaysia, the only tropical country encountering this issue in the world so far. All the world top and brightest scientists are collaborating internationally to reveal the mask behind this ambiguity.'

Her lips looked flickering. 'Although some of them are working on curing SARS spreading speedily around the world, we were still given a helping hand. This is a worldwide crisis. This may have come to the end of the world.'

I was so freaked out when I heard about this. It is traumatized 'What?? What SARS??? Why?? It happened for no reason?? The possibility of the impossible seems to rule like a barbarian.' I just opened up my eyes widely without blinking them while my jaw dropped. As a result, she looked annoyed. When I was about to ask when this absurdity started to happen, she just said like she was a fortune teller, 'It all started to happen three months ago......'

She stopped for awhile.... It may be due to her mulling state of mind. However, she reverted to where she stopped and continued to say, 'I still remember the first warming night I witnessed this to happen was when I was on my way back home in the car after work, I saw it begun with fine snowflakes falling from the sky.'

'At first, I thought it was only some sudden temporary weather changing, I still thought I was lucky enough to witness this before it vanished. Most of the amazed eyes thought it was beautiful. It was because the snowflakes looked like falling stars from the dark sky and fluttering right before falling on the ground. We only wish now it never happened but it seems to have growing soul.......'

She just discontinued what she was saying...... I got a feeling that there is something more, but the conversation ended like that. She just turned around and left me in torment. I know it is never going to be good news. The itchiness of fretfulness just spreads all over me until now.

I can feel the thousands of ant crawling laboriously on my skin that makes me wriggle while my eyes are on the outside, the dismaying but eyed-pleasing picture...... Hopefully, I am wrong about this.....

THE BITTER I WISH TO REMEMBER

<u>7/4/2003</u>

1 It does not seem to vanish

Two weeks have passed. I am still staying in this four wall room while waiting for someone to come and visit me. It is way too comfortable but mind – numbing. I did want to write something on the diary two weeks ago but funnily nothing appeared in my saddening mind.

The weather is getting harder until I can actually see the shovel very often. It can be around three to four times a day on the snowy street across the hospital. This is my first time ever to see a vehicle with shovel in reality! 'erm…..' I think…..

We, Malaysian were used to live in a tropical country. How could ever foresee what is happening now? The shovel is used to remove the snow on the road but a question is asked. A road user would ask 'Is the walkway ensured for travelling safer and easier?'.

A picture of a contractor in the bulky vehicle. He might be who most possibly, is hired by the unknown highest authority to plough snow during the period of high elevation of snow. I did not really see this shovel last week. There were even people driving on the silky road two weeks ago, unlike the soundlessness of this night.

The snowfall is colouring everything in white. The only you can observe. The street is slowly dying. I can rarely find a living creature outside. I stare at the stained lamp post for so long. I guess I just miss the scene. The white pigeon used to be at that usual place.

From the voices revolving around, they were those are working in the hospital. The hired contractor would usually do the snow removal job right before sunrise, but now the frequency of his job has been trebling. It all seems like an upgraded mission.

Their humble opinions ever! The de-icing may be a necessity in latter time. It could not be any better to hinder the formation of the glassy surface on the road. It only shows one thing here: the incrementally decrease of surrounding temperature......

The funny part of them is there is no idea at all on what was heard. However, it seems like no one is keen to find out what de-icing actually is. The arrangement of fate is revealing the answer.

A senior nurse. She was from Seoul. What she unravelled was that action of curbing is merely a process of withering current snow, ice of frost from roadway in elsewhere or any surface, which people need it for travelling.

It may be either in both mechanical means by way of plowing or scraping. A chemical application of salt or other ice-melting chemicals may be needed for some occasions. For example, during the beginning of a storm, it may be used for the sake of precluding or slowing down the production of ice, or the adhesion of slippery particles to the surface.

It is addressed as anti-icing. The precaution what people normally see during the pre-stage of winter time in her hometown! Besides that, brine or wet salt may also be applied swiftly for an effective success before a snow storm hits the town.

If everything is done perfectly well, it will save the penny in your pocket fundamentally. Only reasonable amount of salt used. It thereby allows easier removal by mechanical methods.

The major concern we have to take note is vital. The de-icing of roads with snowplows or dump trucks. Although it is more than affordable for humongous quantity, salt water still freezes at −18 °C. It is still troublesome if the temperature falls below this limitation.

'It is because of the scientific rationale. We should not leave the excessive residue of salt on roads like that. As it normally reacts with steel, when they are coupled up. It will cause long term effect of chemical reaction as to decomposition on most of the vehicles, rebar in concrete bridges and even the environment.'

It was an explicit explanation. I felt thankful. However, I started to understand what was beautiful for me does not exist in reality. I know the beautiful picture has its actual encountered problems in the particular countries. I guess there is a price for everything you own. It is never meant to ignore the merits on one side whereas the downsides on the other side.

I am watching over how the shovel can actually be removing snow now. It is kind of interesting to observe the contractors working in the way I never saw before. On the basis that, it makes me forget something I wish to remember for awhile.

The employed contractor is holding a hand shovel and walking behind a snow blower and heavy front-end loader. When the snow blower starts to function, he will push the snow by way of plowing it to the roadside.

He is walking exhaustively as I can tell from what he feels. I am terrified for a sudden when he almost tripped. My body becomes straight for a moment, and eventually he falls. The blower faces him. He is fluttering the snow. He is like having difficulty to breathe. The vehicle stops as he falls. The driver comes up to him and takes the blower away. He is then coughing.

The driver sounds like whispering. He then grabs his hand and holds him up from the ground. The journey continues.

They make up my grateful feeling. No denial about the responsibility to make sure the road is available for transport. The level of worry is intensifying as I see the snow accumulating considerably high on the pavement. This is going to be burdensome for pedestrian to walk by roadside. However, some of them seem not to be bothered by this issue.

The road is now visible again after snow plowing. Just that I just don't see the legendary performance of anti-icing process yet.

As far as I concerned, would it be easier if the anti-icing is carried out after the snow removal work, wouldn't it? So they would not have to do snow plowing as frequent as they did today. I am thinking that is it because of they don't have the sufficient materials for that purpose…… After all, this is the very first time we are going through this.

The condition is worsening. I still don't know where she is right now……

I am worried. I miss her freckles, wrinkled hands and so on…… The bitter I never want to forget……

2 The bitter I wish to remember

A week ago, due to the ground that, I really wished to find out who is my rumoured family. I decided to make a phone call to her. So, I went to the front counter where the nurse in-charged would generally sit at.

I asked the nurse whose face was new to me. Whether I could get my family contact number and could she help me out to contact her because I did not have coins with me to use public phone to call.

She was nice enough to me and flipped through the patient's personal information record book, eventually she found it. She then dialled the phone number. While waiting for the pick up, I had a glance on the book on the desk. I saw 'The patient's name: Angela Goi as well as the guardian's name: Bectrica Jacob'. The headache just attacked me again...

I tried to hold myself from passing out before the phone was actually got through. She just told me that nobody was answering the phone. I gave a few attempts in every hour after that. However, I was only getting disenchanted for another few times. She was kind enough as to my annoyance.

During the last drilling shot, when I was about to go back to my ward, I stepped on my left slipper and was stumbling. I then fell on the heatless floor.

I just fainted for no reason I could know. I was in coma for five days, and then only woke up. The principal doctor I am used to consult came in on the day I woke up from coma. Its volatility really frightened him up, he said. He was terrified that I would be at an endangered state of health. I was like a living dead person. No matter how hard the nurse called me, I got no response at all even though my heart was still pounding at that time.

I guess I was lucky enough to escape from the purgatory for the second time. However, if I looked at the bright side, it would be something productive as part of my memory had recovered. At the time of the unconscious state, the old days that I spent my time with grandma had been playing in my mind. It was like a flashback.

I remember it all now on how I got this diary from her; how happy I was when I first received it, and how she always woke me up from sleep just to send me to school.

Nonetheless, I also see the picture in weltered memory that I had yelled at she for some undiscovered reasons. I really feel melancholy sick every time I think about it. It must be something unpleasant I forgot but I wish to remember right now. I really almost lose hope. I don't know what else I can actually do to find her back.

I did tell the doctor about my recovery of part of my memory. He just congratulated me that it was good news as my brain seems to reconstitute its ability. He looked at my medical body checkups while talking with me. I guess he is just so good in multitasking until he has to do it every time he examines his patients.

He told me that he still has to make me stay here for a few weeks more for medical examination, to ensure my condition is stable enough The passing out circumstance will not be repeating again, then I can only be discharged. He added on to say: 'This is the third chance that has been given to you to live, so please make good use of it. I know you have been in the state of trepidation, as you can't seem to find your family and therefore your inconsistent emotion will affect your recovery, so remember you are not that lucky next time.'

He was more like warning rather than advising. I just felt uneasy as to what he said. I was grumbling inside me while he was continuing to say the thing he thought he needed to say. I thought that I would never want things to happen in a disturbing way. It was so unfair to blame myself for my own safety while it was a purely accident.

I never expected this to come. How would I know like I was a fortune teller? I know I am fully responsible of the consequences as a result of my behaviour. However, it was not anything ravaging, mischief neither damage of deprivation. I was lonely scared by my own. I just wanted to find her back. I am worried about her safety.

3 No clue on the missing person

I did my best effort to beg the same nurse today, whereby she would make the call on my behalf to grandma. I just did not care whether it would only be another feeling of displeasure of the non-fulfilment of my anticipation. I still wanted to try despite what the doctor said.

The nurse said, 'I am sorry, still the same.' When I heard what she said, it was really tearing me apart even I knew it would end up like this. I held my tears in until I went back to my room. I started crying silently on the ground that I really did not want to make them dissuade about my depression.

It just came to me like that as I started to realise. How wrong I was to mistreat her, the most important person in my life. I wished I could go back to the time before I got knocked down by the vehicle and tell her I am sorry. I hope I would be given a chance to do this..

'Owning is forgettable, losing is regrettable'

Now I know......

However, I have to stay strong as I know I can't just stay in the hospital forever. This mysterious confusion must be resolved one day even though it may not be now.

THE WONDROUS LIGHT
THAT 'GOOSE' BRINGS

<u>21/4/2003</u>

1 The unbearable sign

The same time, the same place, the same author, but not the same weather......
The snow has stopped since this afternoon but still it is a raw weather like the air warmer was not on. Indeed, it is not turned on. Lack of warmer clothes to be put on. So, I can only hide in my bed with my cotton made, thick blanket covering me up. I can hear my bed shivering. Trust me. It is no exaggeration.

I look out of the window. The moon tonight is extraordinarily large that shines wondrous light. I am rubbing my eyes to see what is a hallucination or not. As I see an angel who is wearing a bright nimbus. It also seems like a talking moon which tells me that what a delightful night. I hereby wonder is this just another beautiful lie.

It shines so bright until the cloud in the sky of the night becomes visible in the dark. The cloud looks like a cluster of fluffy white cotton I remember. The wiped my wound after every extraction of my blood as blood sample for medical check-up purposes. It is all clear tonight in the sky. I guess the stars are just too shy to come out after witnessing the brightness of the moon.

In this quiet night, the hired service contractors come again at this time as they have came thrice. They still speak in muted tone. There are quite a number of them. Two of them are in-charged of snow removing by making use of the snow blower on the truck. It is to blow off the snow and make the other worker's job easier by plowing snow.

The other two at the back there are performing distinctive scope of job though it just looks no different at all. There is one on the truck which bears a moderately long tube like a blower at the front of the truck, but unlike the truck at the front. There is something coming out from the tube. The sound of blowing is getting weaker but they left something behind from the tube.

The things look like white sand in countless quantities. The other guy at the back of this truck is using a spade to spread the 'sand' equally. I am thinking that could it be the said 'anti-icing' process. It seems plausible to fit the description that the senior nurse made as to the work of 'anti-icing'. If it is true, the white sand I see will be amazingly salt.

Despite that, I still see a giant lorry behind them. There is an open-air, big container on the lorry. It is moving feebly like it is going to break down soon, in the meanwhile, there are two persons levelling off the snow at the pavement and putting it on the lorry's container. I am asking myself 'is this the way they are removing the excessive residue salt on the road??'

As this is the first time they are performing 'anti-icing' here, I just have so many questions in mind by witnessing how they do it. I also spotted something abnormal about the workers. I have been observing them at the first time they started working. However, they wear something like laboratory masks to work today unlike the previous time.

I am wondering that 'Is it a bad sign to show that the weather has turned worse than before until they can't actually breathe naturally with the assisted device? Is this the reason why the medical officer never allowed me to go outside? I really should not be confounded just because I always got rejected when I mentioned my quest to go outside and I would even get scolded, by Fazlim.'

2 The loathsome in the mirror I endure

Fazlim, my principal good looking doctor. I just found out his name last week. He went into my ward on that day. As usual, he just did all the medical examination that he should have done. He said to me, 'I think it is about time to unwrap your wound. I am so sorry to let you know that we had to cut it all off by reason of the surgery.'

I was shocked, 'What? Do you mean... my... Oh MY GOD! How could it be possible that I don't even know about it??' He continued to say, 'But the hair should grow by now. Don't worry. Time will heal. So, don't get depressed of what you see later.' After his words, he just asked me to hold my head down to unwrap the bandage.

When he started to take off the bandage, my heart was beating strongly but I saw no cliff in front of me to jump off. I also knew that hair will still grow as the metabolism rate of my body should still be compatible at the age of fourteen. Nevertheless, I still felt nervous about this unexpectedly, unreasonably acceptable news.

I remember that the age of my long floating hair was as old as my age. I never really cut them short. It was tremulously unforeseeable that I was cut bareheaded on the last four months. The pain was drenching over my heart for a minute to mourn. I felt so long for him to take off the bandage though he did not feel the same as I did.

I did not want to open my eyes as I was too scared to find out how I would look like with fuzzy short hair. He saw my hilarious response with my eyebrows frowned. He just took a small piece of paper and started folding. I was too curious to close my eyes anymore, so I just opened them and looked at what was he doing.

'A goose'. That was he folded. He smiled to me and spoke, 'Here is Fazlim who wishes to give you this goose as a gift. Don't ever underestimate this goose. It is not just a paper goose; instead, it is a lucky goose. It brings you fortune and luck. Here, take it. My sister used to give me this lucky goose when she thought I needed it the most.'

The moment I saw this paper goose which I am holding right now, I was stunned. As I felt like I had received something like this before. The memory was so blur. I did not even know if it was real or not but I could tell its risibility was existed. It was not something I read in this diary but it was from my past.

I am pretty sure that there was someone giving this goose to me before. I tried to think hard to make myself remember what I have forgotten. Still, it was a failed attempt. Luckily, I did not have to go through the torturing fearful headache. At that time, I was thinking that this lucky goose really works.

I still felt wondered about my new look in spite of how Fazlim comforted me, though the fear and anxiety that ran through my veins was extremely annoying. After he went out, I rushed to the private toilet in my ward and took a look in the mirror. Oh my god, I just could not believe what I saw in the mirror.

My long brown curly hair was all gone. I looked exactly like a hip-pop rapper whose hairstyle is like separated spirals with fair skin. I confused about my genitality. I did not seem right to see my hair like this. I was not used to look like this. I struggled in front of the mirror for a few hours by standing there and staring at the one in the mirror.

Slowly, I started to adore the one I stared at. I guess I could not keep complaining about my hair right now because I would not survive and have a chance to stare at the one in the mirror if my hair was not shaved and hence, I did not even go through the operation.

So, I just told myself that every cloud has a silver lining. I can only look at the bright side. At least, I will still be able to see my hair to grow long. I did later try to find the scar of the successful battle but it was like disappearing in time. Perhaps, it just wanted to hide from me so that I would not be reminded of the thing I should never forget.

3 A new friend for the day

I really miss my grandma. I still have not given up on finding her. I still go to the same counter and ask the same nurse for the determined favour even though I never succeeded. I am wondering if she is okay in this hard winter. I have not seen her for four months. Where has she been?? I pray to the god in my heart, 'Please make her come back to me safely, please….' Thinking about this, the tears are wobbling in my eyes.

However, I still had something pleasant that put a smile on my paper like face today. I went out from my room today to make phone call as usual. I felt that the people working were getting lesser. I just ignored this weirdness for a while to make call. After I made a vain phone call to grandma, while I was looking down to the floor, I accidentally ran into someone who I did not normally see. Her pale sad looking face told me that she was a weak angel that fighting hard against the devil cells in her body.

I directly apologised towards my carelessness. She just smiled at me until I could see a dimple on her right cheek. She said, 'It is ok, it was my fault too that I did not really look properly before I walked.' Some unknown reason invoked me to introduce myself to her.

I was really glad that I could as I said with shyness, 'Hi, I am Angela. What's your name?' She replied, 'Hi, nice to meet you, my name is Kasani. I am Indian. Are you an Indian too??' I laughed and said, 'I am a mixed Australian and Malaysian.' We started conversing like old friends. I guess we were making loud noises by laughing and giggling at the jokes we made.

The nurse walking by had chased us back to our wards separately. We just kept nodding our head with no intended agreement. We were rebellious enough to pretend like we were walking back towards our wards individually. However, we sneaked into her room secretly to continue our own sweet girls' chatting time as a result of the invitation she made. Her ward is just five room distance away from mine.

In her private ward, I could tell she has been staying here for quite some time. As I see so many clothes and jackets hanging over in a closet she had in her ward where I don't even have one. She told me that her parents bought her all these things. Her parents would normally visit twice every two days.

Unfortunately, due to the snowfall, it makes her parents having difficulty to come over here by car. Furthermore, they are living in the land across the sea. It would be inconvenient for them. Coming here all the time needs consistent effort to balance. She explained that her parents are not superman. Human is vulnerable, they will feel tired too. So, they won't come here as often as they usually did.

She also said that she always goes out of her room to wander along the corridor, whenever she feels bored. This was the first time she met someone like her today. I knew who she was mentioning about though she did not say it out. It would be nice to make new friend here, otherwise, I would not have anyone to talk to. As most of the people I met here was extremely busy.

ESCAPE PLAN

30/4/2003

1 Planning to escape

The question that I have been analysing for all these while: How I am going to enforce this? I can't stay here in peace while she might be in danger outside. I need to go out from here and find her. I know my wish will never be granted. The wish could only exist in my mind like forever if I continued to talk with no action. Furthermore, an excuse of medical observation is frequently utilised.

Additionally, I do not even have the ability to pay off the eye popping bill when I am just wearing a dress with no pocket at all. On the ground that, grandma is my legal guardian. I will never have the right to touch a single penny until the age of validity. So, I wonder how to escape from the monetary responsibility.

None of the things in my mind is morally faultless. I would not have thought about it unless it was necessity. In the critical situation, the wrongful decision may not be culpable though it is never right. As a conclusion, I need to get out from here somehow. I got a bad feeling about what is happening now on her. No explanation can be made in respect of this feeling based on the fact of its intuitive nature.

I have been waiting patiently. Improvement of health is needed as the first rule to fight is survival. So, Survival under this frosty weather is slightly possible. I did ask Fazlim about my case. He was also impressed by the speed of my recovery. He got awarded compliments by most of the medical experts who originally did not agree to perform the surgery on me. They never thought he would be the success among the unattainability.

I guess there must be a reason for keeping me alive. She will definitely be part of it. The wound on my head is already healed. As I can only see the three inches long scar when I am showed by the nurse who holding the mirror high behind my head and I am looking into the front mirror simultaneously. I do not usually request for this rear view mirroring.

Pleasantly, I don't get headache as much as I did before. Part of the missing puzzles have been discovered. Although I have still been trying hard, it is a profound recovery to me.

From what I remember in the memory, I am never a sporty person. I never actively participated in any sport activity during my younger age. Suprisingly, I still can recall the history record of my primary school year where the whole class was obliged to go trying the sport programme which was held by the school.

I remember how the 100m short run paralyzed my legs. I ran fast in the name of effort. I was still the last in the list from the beginning until the end of the race. It would only a yearning for failure, even though there was only one choice. It is also because I can get tired very easily, even if I am getting involved in light physical exercise.

However, I must still go to save her even I may not be qualified to. This is the only thing I can do to compensate her lost love. Hence, I have to take a risk. This is not the place where I belong to. I just need to run out from this comfort cage and go back to my house to investigate or interrogate if possible.

It is really a regret to think of staining my white shirt like that while I still have to wear it. However, I know it is not the best time to mourn for the loss. Therefore the issues I have identified are: Firstly, how to get out from here without them noticing; secondly, how to recognise my way back home safely under such raw weather; thirdly, I need thick coats and some clothes to wear in spite of this hospital gown.

My plan is this operation should be initiated at night time especially during the time the hired contractors are performing their jobs. It is brilliant. As the time comes, what I need the most is unpleasant sounds. I can actually hear the noise even if I am in the room and the window is all well-closed. The nurses in night shift hereby are rarely distracted by the potential noise I might make during escape time.

As long as they are concentrating on some other things, I could be ensured sneaking safely out from my room. So, I am thinking about the solution to this question while I am writing and looking out of the window again to observe the condition of the road tonight. Last few weeks ago, I could still see a few pedestrian walking on the shiny pavement but the street is more like an abandoned field nowadays.

2 A winter desert

I can remember that there was a beautiful meadow right opposite this hospital. Nevertheless, beauty never last. What I observe now is not what I was used to see. It is the creepiest thing you can't tell. The street is so abnormally quiet.

Its vacancy is never a good sign in this small town. As there is no more needle penetrating my thin walled cells, I can actually have freedom in making any movement. So, I get up from my bed and walk to the window, after I see the window sashes.

It is like I can hear rustling from the window, calling me to go near it and open it while I am holding this diary in my hand. I just think I may still be able to feel the air flow even if the red light is shown.

I first put down the diary on the floor and use my both hands to pull up the window sashes by way of travelling up on tracks. I think probably because of the unforeseen changes of surrounding temperature and also the humidity in the air, the sashes may have warped.

If this is the case, I will never open the window successfully, even though I have put in all the available strength inside me to open it.

The window is still remained closed. It may also because the window is painted shut. If it is the issue, I doubt that whether it is plausible to get the window opened as this hospital was built on 1973. Presumably, it will never be possible to open the window if it has never been opened.

I have thought of getting a sharp blade to segment the frame and sash but I don't have any of those offensive devices. While thinking about this sticky window, I have made use of all I have to wrench and in the meanwhile, I push the window with my slightly tubby shoulder. I am not sure if it is helpful but I just do it anyway. I feel the instant coldness by touching the glass.

I also speculate that the difference of temperature inside the room and cold weather outside the window may be the cause for this difficulty in opening window anyhow. After a few industrious attempts, my effort is finally paid off. The sashes have moved up arduously. I get irritated by its sliding sound effect. The biting wind flow is blown at me for a sudden. I can really feel the horribly enormous difference after the window is opened.

I quickly pull down the sashes of the window, before the possibility that I may catch a cold. There is snowflake sticking on my right arm. I am stunned for a second while I feel fairly cold for a while just because of this microscopic snowflake. I am moving my left hand towards it to try picking it up. It is all in slow motion.

When I just start touching even before I pick it up, it turns out of shape and then my fingertips feel faintly wet. It is just gone like that. I just think snow is composed of water molecule. At this time, I have been reminded of what my primary school science teacher who taught me as to how snow is born in the first place.

3 Snow is not just snow

So far as I remember, snow is the product of the condensing process. It is found in the form of flakes of crystallised water. It will fall from a thousand feet high clouds. In other words, snow is usually formed when water vapor is changed directly to ice particle, up high in the atmosphere without first going through the conversion of being liquid, before falling to the ground.

On the other hand, I think the snowflake I saw just now is actually ice – crystal. Snowflake has six side and also two hundred of ice crystal particles. We may be confused but snowflake and snow are scarcely distinctive. The ice – crystal of the snowflake is actually comprised of small components of dirt that exists in the atmosphere as a result of wind blow.

However, the question is what makes all these happen. As what had usually been comprehended, the earth's axis is titled approximately 23°. This only affects the more northern and southern latitudes are also included.

Due to the reason that, sunlight only strikes the earth at a lower angle, and hence, the earth radiates more heat than it receives. Therefore, the temperature of the affected area will be reduced significantly and so, this contributes to the natural phenomena of snowfall fundamentally.

Malaysia is famously known to be a tropical country because of its geographic coordinate. It does have the same four seasons in a year as the tropical weather does not change much throughout the years. Although the weather in Malaysia may be influenced by the seasonal monsoon, the weather here does not provide extremities even if it may cause unpleasant flood here sometimes.

4 The changing revelation

'What has changed the weather here?' The more mysterious it is, the more I want to check it out....

By thinking about this issue, I swear I will really lose my sleep during the late night. So, I decide to go to see Kasani even though she may be sleeping at this time. I am lurking behind the door of my room with the door slightly opened. I stand at the back of the door and wait for the nurse to walk away from the counter she is now sitting there.

She eventually gets up from the chair and walk towards the opposite direction of where my room is located. It's time. I quickly walk out from the room, and close the door delicately, continue walking to Kasani's room. When I reach her room, I just open the door quietly and get inside her room.

5 The sleeping beauty

As what I speculated, she is sleeping right now. I feel so down as I feel mean to wake her up while she will feel tired easily. However, I just laid my eyes on her for a while, the feeling of sympathy creeps in. As a result of suffering from anemia, she is just a teenage girl who can only live in her dreams in a limited reality.

There are too many things she wishes to do based on that reason. She told me before that, she loves long hair, and she was used to keep her hair long at knee length but on the basis of having suffered this sickness, she had to cut her hair short to prevent severe hair loss.

Her dark, long healthy hair had become short, delicate and lesser in volume if it was compared with last time. For now, she has to wear wig for covering up the unwanted foreseeability. I am really impressed by her positive attitude that she could still make a joke about this. According to her, it is like gold dust as not many people could experience in changing as many hair styles as she wants.

There is nothing else I can try out now, but something changes me when I am too desperate to think at that time. When I turn around, I see the white wooden cupboard which is wide-opened. I see jackets in different colours, blouses, long cotton made trousers, knee-length socks, as well as those boots that also fits my feets.

I turn around and look at the sleeping beauty. She looks absolutely stunning on the small bed. An adorable girl who is just one year younger than me; our body sizes and the heights are all almost the same. I just think it may be a bestowed opportunity. It is because it will soothe my plan by having these settled in part.

Since she is apparently not enabled to be making discussion with me, I will have to go back to my room and have a good rest for the preparation of my 'escape plan'......

The smirk I then see in the mirror. I just know that I have made up my mind to incriminate her to get involved in my plan.....

WHAT A PLAN!!!!

<u>1/5/2003</u>

1 Plan A – Get what you need in hand

Today was the best day to make my planned intention work. It was because of most of the staffs in the hospital were taking leave on this Labour Day which was also a well-deserved public day. Fazlim was also not in today as I did not see him come over to have my medical examination done on time in this morning.

I quietly stood behind the door and observed the corridor. It was all in silence. The staff nurses would generally be busy walking along the corridor but fortunately, not for today. It was a tranquil day. I could only see two working nurse stay in the counter in front there today. Although they looked kind of disconsolate, I was thinking to myself at this moment that 'Is god also granting me a golden chance for executing my escape plan? Thanks God!! Sorry for those who were still working on holiday.'

So, I just sneaked out of my room to Kasani's room, while the nurses were doing their work and in the meanwhile, they seemed now pretty enjoy chatting with each other, like they are on public holiday now in their workplace, after they have distributed the medicines to the patients individually. I guess I am right. They didn't really notice what I was doing now, and hence I just walked steadily to the right along the corridor and headed on Kasani's room.

Kasani seems to be very surprised to see me open the door of her ward. Kasani rolled her glittering eyes and said: 'How dare you scare me like that??' I hummed: 'Shhhhhhh…….. Can you speak slowly?? Loud noise will make them notice the intrusion. I am so sorry but I have to. I seriously need your help.'

Kasani asked 'What is it??' I illustrated to her: 'As I told you earlier, I need to go find my grandma. However, I need to first get out from here.' Kasani was thrilled and then she answered, 'So, you need me to assist you. Oh, yeah!!! I am going with you!!! Take me with you!!!' 'What!! No way!! You gonna stay here as it is too dangerous outside. I will be going by my own.' I opposed to her suggestion strongly.

Kasani felt like she was thwarted by my insistence and said 'You should look at the sky today, the weather is bleak. I feel worried about them too. I have not gone back home for one and a half year. I am home sick. I have not seen my parents for months. I miss them as much as you miss her. Why you have to be so mean??'

She then started sobbing. I released my extended breath and stopped her crying by saying to her that 'Okay. Alright. Let me consider about this in ten minutes time.' I looked the small mole on the right side of her forehead while I spotted a tape recorder on the desk.

Thinking about if...... If I brought her with me, what about her medical needs?? I would not know how to save her if anything bad was incurred as a consequence of the unwelcoming harsh weathers. On the other hand, if I did not bring her along, she might just stay in this limited room like forever and ever in spite of she might be able to recover in latter time.

This isn't a frayed hope, is it? So,.....

She saw me got upset as my face was being wrinkled. She said, 'I know what you are worrying about... Just be steady.... I will bring my own spare medication prescribed by my doctor to stimulate my body to control the in-house devil.'

She held my hand. I felt the coldness with desire. She continued, 'Moreover, I still can't seem to find a suitable blood stem cell donor for me to undergo the transplantation of blood and marrow stem cell in a vein of my chest.....

I don't want to die here. Please. I seriously know how to take care of myself.. Please bring me with you so that we can hold on each other.' I could tell that she was too determined to be precluded. So, I just brought her in.

I told her about my plan and waited for the late night to come ...

2 Plan B Get ready to move

I got myself wore the clothes and wardrobe with a piece of knitted scarf on my neck that she lent and I told her to do the same. What a long night. I was waiting for Kasani to come over my room as my room was nearer to the staircase which I thought it was more appropriate to escape by way of using the stairway. I thought she would be here by now after having the tape recorder setting up. I hoped that she would make it on time right before the hired contractors came.

I was standing at the back of the door while waiting for her. I observed the nurses were walking to the left and going into a ward to the other side. At this time, I saw Kasani running speedily towards my direction but she hit on a trolley left along the corridor. I could hear the nurses were mentioning about the noise coming out from the other side. My heart was beating hard until I could actually hear it.

I sneaked out of my room swiftly in order to ease my plan to escape while I tried to communicate with her without making any sound. So, she could hurry up in running to the stairway right away before they walked out and ruined our plan. Right about now, I heard loud noises. I listened carefully and I found out it was the service trucks. I told myself it was the time.

I beckoned to her, she seemed to understand my signal. She ran to me like crazy in spite of the noises she made might wake others up. Finally, she got here. I just held her hand and ran down the stairs. When we reached the ground floor, we were so happy until we kept jumping up and down in the hallway at the ground floor there.

My bad to be reckless. I guess the noises we made had made the security guard who has grizzly hair, aware of some night invaders. We realised someone coming from the side door. We walked inaudibly to the back of the decoration tree and hid there. A considerably elderly man walked into the hallway and used torchlight to irradiate the hall with his right hand and a lengthy gun on his left hand.

He was alert.....

I guess he could not discover anything, he hereby went off after checking the front door. 'It was locked. He must be guarding the side door, the only way out.' I said to Kasani. Kasani blinked her eyes for a few times, by telling that she would distract the guard. I immediately held her hand before she went off.

I said, 'Please stay calm Kasani, otherwise we all would be caught. We have first to make sure whether this Mr. Guard is all alone or he has a company. I pulled her hand so that she would follow me at my back. We were creeping into the other side which is nearer to the side entrance.

We were lying against the wall while I kept peeping pryingly over the guard and observing carefully the environment surrounding us. I could already feel a cold breeze on my face and at the same time, he nearly dozed off as I could see his head was nodding repeatedly. Hence, I just told Kasani to move mutely along with me.

3 Almost there

When we almost reached the exit, we could actually get out from here. The closer we got to the exit, the more we felt the cool harsh air. Suddenly, Kasani sneezed obstreperously. It really scared me off. Not just because of the loud sneeze, it was also due to the reason the guard might be awakened. I just held her hand and ran rapidly. It happened like a launched rocket.

After we had arrived at the front gate, he abruptly had his eyes opened completely and stood up to look around with nettled eyes. We just ran without looking back. Despite the frosty weather, we did not really feel frozen because of the needs of the high metabolism rate as we were running violently. What a cheeky night as we were treacherous!

After running across the streets, we stopped and took a rest for a while, because of the exhausted state. I looked behind, and I could only see an empty street. I just thought where we got our guts from. Most of the streetlights were not working whereas the intact was too dim. Some of them were flashing. If there was no dazzling moonlight I could never see a thing.

Kasani might think the darkness scared us the most but she never knew she missed a little bit about the fact. The fact that what makes you feel the fear is the uncertainty in the darkness. We then stopped resuming to run. There was evaporation coming out from her mouth. So, I wondered.

As the sky was bizarrely clear tonight, there was no snowfall but only fairly strong wind. I could also hear dogs bow-wowing at this night but I could not even see their shadows.

All the shop outlets were closed. I could not even feel a breath on the street except us. When my eyes were on the ground, it was all full of snow. I could also feel them sinking whenever I moved my feet. I could only see my boots were partially covered by the snow. It was like I was standing in the middle of the quicksand in white.

I could actually measure the depth of the snow by using my covered hand. With a rough estimation, it was about ten centimetres deep from the ground. Despite that, whenever I was marching by lifting my feet up and down. I could actually hear the sound of scrubbing cornstarch or salt, and I could scarcely feel the snow squeaking while I walked upon, probably because of the crushing of the ice-crystals within snow.

During the break, Kasani told me that she already started to feel wintry. So, I just asked her to keep walking as there was still a long journey to go back to my home as well as her. I just thought we might not feel as arctic as we felt right now when we were walking. As we walked further, we felt bizarrely creepier. I did not know what had gone wrong but I just felt that way.

4 The right shoulder tapping angel

Suddenly, I felt someone tapping my right shoulder. It freaked me out. I was too scared until I screamed it out with my eyes closed. When I started to calm myself down, I first squinted and then only gradually opened my eyes. I only realised Kasani was missing. 'Where is Kasani?? Kasani!!! Kasani!!!'

When I turned around, I saw Kasani lying in the snow, she looked bleached, like a sleepy vampire. I momentarily supported her head with my bare hand with no gloves on. I put her in my arms so that she would feel a little bit warmer. I then scanned around to see whether there was a safely nice place to hide in.

At this time, I could hear someone's footsteps on this cold fluffy ground and also see a source of light. I saw someone walking towards our direction. I waved at that person so that that person might lend his helping hand on us. When he came closer, I saw a face in my long lost neighbourhood. As our eyes met, I knew he lived in my past. The familiar face I stared but I just could not recall who he was even if I tried toughly to think. However, it was still unfathomably unresolved.

He found me and Kasani in the snow with the powerful torchlight he was holding but he held a reasonably long sharp blade on his hand. I shivered for a second about what I saw. He went up to me and wondered what happened. I just told him the troubling situation without even asking his mysterious identity. Having heard of the severe illness as to Kasani, he immediately bent his knee down and carried Kasani. He led the walk now. 'Follow me.' We continued to walk by going through the steep stairway. The floors were not deadly silent. However, I strangely felt secured here. We eventually reached the small flat.

There was a completely and domestically furnished house in spite of its space and its darkness. There was no one found in this flat unlike what I had anticipated that I might be able to meet anyone else who was also the 'survivor' like us in this unfavourable condition of the night.

He put her down on a long, three person seated sofa, and swiftly went to kitchen to grab her a glass of hot water. He held her head up, and tried to make her sipping the water. Finally, she woke up. I was like feeling a lot relieving now. I am fully responsible of her life now since the second I asked a favour from her. I should have foreseen she would want to follow. I should never let her know.

I could not afford to let her risk herself by allowing her to continue following.

5 Lucas?

He eventually spoke, 'Hi, I am Lucas.....' The moment he mentioned his name, I was shocked. The name 'Lucas' was spinning around in my mind for the night before I could actually fall asleep. So, I spent my night with recording the adventure we went through today after I was satisfied by flipping over the older pages ....

THE LUCKY STAR OF MINE???

<u>2/5/2003</u>

1 The name in my diary

I woke up with a deep breath this early morning before the sunrise while two of them were still sleeping comfortably in the thick blankets that Lucas provided us in two spared rooms. I guess it might be because of the raw weather in this morning. My inhalation and exhalation were rare in this room. The room was infinitesimal in physical size even if I still wore the coat. Unfortunately, it did not make any difference.

As a consequence of waking up early, I could actually hear the whisper of strong wind blow coming from the window. However, it was closed. It was all out of curiosity. Hence, I was walking closer feebly to the louvered window on my left. The cold was incrementally getting biting. It made me forgot about what I was wearing. I momentarily looked down but I did not see the T-shirt on me.

I saw a hole on the glass of the louvered window which mainly permitted the wind to intrude this limited space. I examined the window with my seriousness as if all my attention was attracted by this dusty window. I could tell the hole was possibly incurred by reason of the cleaning process of this window.

After the careful observation over the flawed window, I peeped at the situation outside through this visibly small hole. I saw an advertising paper whirling around like performing a dancing show. The snow was falling to the ground like rainfall. It seemed to be a kind of heavy today.

At this time, I was thinking that it might cause Kasani to catch a cold later. So, I went all over the house except for Lucas's room to find something apt to cover the hole up. Before I found the sticky tape, I spotted some music instruments at the corner in the living room. It was weird. As I thought to myself, I did not even notice them when I first arrived at this house.

There was an unusually excitement that attracted me to go nearer to what I saw, particularly, the guitar. I went closer, had my knee down, and leaned over the guitar. I used my fingers to touch the wood; it was so beautiful though I could tell it was aging. I tried to pick up the guitar, sat on the floor, and put it across my laps. I could not help myself to start playing the guitar. It was all in gentle and delicate so that I would not wake them up.

When I was playing the guitar by strumming the strings on the bridge of the guitar, I felt something extraordinarily rough on the fairly smooth surface of this guitar. I remembered Lucas had used torchlight yesterday and where he kept. I thereby went to take the torchlight to light up. I just want to see what was actually on the guitar's surface.

I eventually found the torchlight to illuminate the surface. I saw 'Angela'. I thought that 'Isn't that my name? Or, someone who shares the same name with me??' 'Hey, you!!! Put your hand off my guitar!!' Lucas shouted. I was too nervous to respond, so I just held the guitar in my hand while standing up.

He rushed to my direction and took the guitar away from me by thrusting me into the corner between the walls. During this moment, I felt the element of elegiac fluttering inside my brain. However, I did not know what was all about, but I could feel its existence. In a sudden, there was something blurry that hit my chaotic brain.

'Lucas.' The name I read before in this diary. I know him personally?? Perhaps, just a stranger who is familiar to me??? One coincidence may be hallucination but how about when there are so many of them?' These were the questions I had in mind when we had an eyeball confrontation. His eyes contained hatred and anguish. He did not seem like he knows me personally. The way he treated me was like a stranger that he hated.

2 The lucky star I previously knew

He apologized, 'I am sorry but can you please don't ever touch my guitar again without my permission. Please.' The way he stared at me was terrifying. I just thought that he was going to kill me with his eyes. I promised him by replying him, 'I am sorry too, I won't lay my hand on it ever again.' I took a bow to him after expressing my apology.

He seemed to have himself calm down a little bit more, so he just sat on the floor as how I did just now and started playing a song as well as singing:

'She is not mine, but you are the only one
Paint my sky with blue and black
At nowhere to start,
Don't know how,
And don't know why.

Oh my girl, you seem so far away
Though we're breathing the same air,
In city we used to live,
I feel close~~,
The fondly distance.

Oh yea~~ this lucky star ~~
I don't care who you are,
I will shine bright
Oh~~~ shine bright.
Even in your blue sky.

This girl, The secret I keep
Days and nights at all the time
Just to think about you.
Come across,
Like I ain't good in tik tak toe.

Oh yea~~~ this lucky star~~~
I don't care who you are,
I will be your lucky star,
Be right there where you are,

I wanna be your lucky star,
Wonder how you are?
Look down at where you are,
Can you see this lucky star.

This lucky star~~
Lucky star~~
Your only lucky star......

The song sounded melancholic. He was tearing. The 'stars' struck on my sympathized eyes and the grief in my heart were intermingling without confusion about what feeling I had now. I tried to walk closer just to comfort him right before two of us heard Kasani yelling. Having heard the monstrous scream, we ran into the room where Kasani was sleeping.

When we arrived at the room with the door opened, I saw Kasani standing right in front of the window. She looked horrified like she saw something startling until she lost her sensibility. Her eyes were fully opened without blinking, her jaw just dropped and her face was like frozen in this hard weather.

I walked near her while calling her name. However, she was totally becoming a deadly object. She gave no response towards my call. Lucas was tailing me at the back there like he was frightened by this unpleasant mutiny by Kasani. The moment I touched her hand she went crazy.

3 The unwelcoming!

She screamed again, 'Run!! Run as fast you can!!! They are coming!!!!' I wondered why she kept repeating the same sentences by asking us to get away from here. Lucas then grabbed my hand as well as Kasani's icy cold hand. He went straight to the drawer to take the knife and also the torchlight, and then pulled us to the front door.

It was like he wanted to move out from here and in the meanwhile, he did not even want to take his guitar. The way he held my hand was too tight. I felt painful on my wrist. He was tilting us to the staircase. At this time, I could hear some wild animals howling. They sounded like they were in hunger for many days, and they were too desperate to eat some fresh juicy flesh.

I was like a brazen little deer. I did not care about Lucas's effort of getting all of us leaving this dangerous place safely and also the roaring of the wild beasts. I was struggling to get Lucas's hand off me and I wittingly wished to go back to the house to take my diary with me, as I urgently needed it every single day to constitute my faith on the scepticism that whether she is alright or not.

After all, it was like a precious diamond that I could only be reminded the thing I wished to remember but unluckily, I had forgotten. When I had the diary with me, I could only feel her existence whenever I held the diary book in hand. However, in this critical situation, there was something else appearing in my head too.

I could not have time to mull. The noises created by the beasts were getting closer to us. I could even tell there must be many of them. I did not care about what the potential danger I was going to self-indulge myself in and the seriousness of the outcome. I requested Lucas to go hiding in a safer place with Kasani.

A fervent voice was heard, 'You two go first. I assure I will catch you two later.' After finished saying what it was supposed to say, I struggled to get rid of Lucas's hand. Finally, I did. I just ran back to the house and got the front door locked. I guess it was due to my nervous disposition, my mind completely went blank. I could not really remember a single thing about where I had placed my diary.

I ransacked all over the house just to find one small piece of book. While I was busy in searching for my diary, I heard the noises outside the front door. It was like someone knocking the door violently. I froze to prevent any further sound for a while. My breath was getting frequently heavier than usual. The noises then vanished.

I just thought they might have gone as they thought there was nothing inside the house. So, I just started to move my right leg. I heard the noises again. It was getting strikingly louder this time. The door was continuously being knocked with strong force. The door literally seemed to be tenuous.

4 The last goodbye

I was utterly caught in the state of timorous temperament. I was entirely freaked out. I knew I had to be decisive in this time, I mulled for awhile though it was like I took three months to think. Still, I eventually decided to go into the room which I slept yesterday and hide.

I ran to the room and locked the door. I even pushed the bed to the door with all my strength, so that they could be averted to come in. However, when I was about to make it, they broke the lock, got the door half-opened, and outstretched their heads to see what was in there.

I saw more than ten stray dogs waiting outside the door to rush in. They did not look as friendly, and affectionate as they were used to be. Instead, they were fierce by showing their ferocious aggressiveness. There were even blood stains on their sanguinary mouths. I guess this might be what Kasani saw just now which made her went insane.

The dog whose got a thin, small scar on its left eyes, eventually got his head in successfully, was a Lancashire Heeler breed. I could only see giant dog breeds but not small dog breeds. I was feeble to go against these dogs. There were too many of them. They could really push the bed away from the door at a slow pace. I knew I would not be able to hold any longer.

Hence, I was searching around the room to see whether there was another exit. I was still wholly despondent. I just closed my eyes as I knew I would not be that lucky at this time. I took out the lucky goose out from the pocket of my jacket with my right hand while my left hand was still holding on the bed with the hope that miracle would happen.

I would really regret that the last goodbye I never told grandma. Thinking about this, I made a long groan and started to whimper melancholy. They were like very exhilarated by my tears as they kept pushing the door. I just thought of giving up at this moment. Suddenly, I heard long, loud, doleful cry uttered by them.

The Lancashire was squeezing its head out from the door, and turning around to inspect what was going on. I then heard the sound of chopping or slaughtering and the sound of howling came in later. I was unwillingly surprised with a feeling of great enthusiasm. I immediately stood up with a grin on my face.

Someone was commanding me to open the door by removing the bed away from the door. I could recognise the voice, 'It was Lucas.' I pulled the bed with all I could although I felt I was not as vigorous as this early perilous morning. As I did not think I would have replaceable energy now, he tried to assist me by pushing the door opened.

He was a tubby teenage boy. He could push the door opened within just a few second intensively.

I literally fell on the ground. I was lying on the floor with my face looking up the ceiling. Luckily, the jacket was thick enough to prevent friction between the fragile nature of my skin with the floor. I did not feel much pain.

I felt my palm was touching something. I got myself up and took a look at it. 'It is my diary!!!' I was laughing. It was ear-splitting. I could not believe it. I finally found it!!! My diary that was given by my grandma!! I could not hold my tears any longer, I burst into tears unexpectedly.

Lucas woke me up from my bubble dream by saying, 'Hey! It is not the time to cry like a baby girl. Get up. Hurry. Before they find us here. We have to go now.' By hearing what he said, I got up from where I fell undoubtedly.

He helped me to remove the bed and eventually the door could be opened, so that there would be enough space for to get out from the room. Nevertheless, I felt wet on my right palm. I hereby took a look on my hand.

It was red fishy blood. My hands were shaking. I thought, 'I am hurt?'. Lucas tapped on my right shoulder, 'It is not yours.' I saw his right arm bleeding. 'Oh my god!! You are hurt.' He was calm enough to comfort me by telling me that it would be alright.

Finally, we got out from the room, but the scene I saw was too traumatically horrible in the sense that it was bloodily unforgettable. It reminded me of how I witnessed my parents died as a result of the fatal accident. I really felt like vomiting. I was giddy and was about to faint by reason of the sanguinary smell.

5 The feeling where the electric current wass running through my blood

Lucas leaned to my right side and caught me before I fell onto these corpses. Lucas said, 'Hey! Are you alright??' I replied vigorously, 'Yea. I am okay as long as I don't see all these lying on the floor like the dishes for my dinner.' Lucas just supported me by putting my arm around his shoulder while we were walking away from there simultaneously. The way we walked like we were twins.

He put me down on the couch. He went to the other side of direction. I was waiting with fearful patience. He eventually came out with a bottle of disinfectant and bandage. He was prepared to be swathed. I decided to help him. It was awfully heart-breaking as a result of my insistence. I whispered, 'Thank you.', but he heard me and we were staring at our hopeful eyes.

He woke me by saying, 'Kasani is still waiting up there. Hurry up. Let's go.'

While heading to the front door, I turned my head back and looked at the guitar which had my name on it. Lucas then stopped walking forward. He said, 'The guitar is not so convenient to be brought along. I have to leave it here though I don't want to. I promise that I will come back to get it if we survive in this cold war.'

I was like getting nervous shock which caused me forgot on how to speak. I was thinking that whether he was smart or he knew me extremely well to this extent. Was that obvious for him to know what I wanted to do through my demeanour even if there was no advance communication revealed. We then kept on walking out of the front door and locking the door before we walked off. It was an abnormal scene but I guess he was worried.

He led me up the stair without collaborating me anymore. Before that, when he was about to let go my hand by moving my wrist away from his shoulder, I was like electrified. The cells in my body were stimulated like I could feel them shivering. I knew it was kind of exaggerating but it was really how I felt.

While walking up the stair, I was thinking about this question at the same time like I just forgot what the dangerous action scene I had been through within an hour ago. We went three floors up and he stopped at level seven. He went into a garbage room which all the waste disposal would be dumped here.

The smell was literally unpleasant. I saw Kasani squatting at the corner of the wall there. The moment she saw me. 'You are alive!' She was too happy, until I could actually see her big eyes were smiling. She ran to me and gave me a big hug. She said, 'I am glad that you are fine.'

I replied, 'I am so sorry to make you two worried. It is my bad....' Lucas interrupted, 'This is not the time to question who is at fault but all we need is working together to win this battle in the cruel hard war.' Kasani frowned as she saw the fresh wound on Lucas's arm, 'You are hurt?!' Lucas answered, 'It is not the matter now.' Kasani and me agreed about what he said by nodding our heads like there was no way to stop it.

I tried to clarify everything so I asked Lucas, 'What is actually going on right now??' Lucas answered, 'Do you mean the dogs or the weather??' I replied, 'I don't understand both as I was in coma last few months ago. It has already been in this way when I woke up.'

6 The disastrous 'wonderland'

Lucas explicitly demonstrated, 'I also don't know why it is happening. It all started five months ago. I never expected a gentle snowfall would become a disastrous winter storm in the consecutive months. Many domestic houses were wholly ravaged. The unsupportive roofs and the heavy weight of the accumulating snow. As a consequence, the house collapsed......'

The grief on his face I could see. It was all remained in sadly silence. He held on and continued, 'All the agricultural plants had frayed because of this harsh weather and not even the domestic livestock were surviving. The condition here is no longer suitable for human or any living creature to live.'

I broke his explanation by saying, 'Now I see why… and the dogs!'

He continued, 'It is not the end of the story yet…… Most people who are financially capable. They choose to leave this country as fast as they still can. On the ground that, it is clear to foresee based on what is happening right now. This will be our future. For those who stayed, it would only be unfortunate.'

'All the general transportation were disrupted. The water transportation like boats which contained goods were stuck in the sea because of the frosty weather and it was also unable to unload as well. This raw weather also made air and road transportation impossible to work out.'

I seemed to get the picture, and hence said, 'So, this is how all these blockage to the accessibility of this island led to food shortage.' 'Yes. Additionally, worst things never stopped. The electricity supply as well as water supply had also been blocked out during last night. It is going to be all in dark at night from now on. I guess it would also be the same for the rest of the states.'

Lucas went on saying, 'The domestic or commercial pets, especially like dog which is stronger and aggressive than any other domesticated animals here, have changed their gastronomical nature from omnivore to carnivore. I had witnessed it by myself yesterday.….'

He held his head down. He forcefully continued to say, 'I guess the surviving dogs could not hold themselves from the devil call of hunger. The innocent weaker dogs were the scarification. I saw. It was merciless I knew they were going to attack any warm-blooded living creature. All they ever know now is to satisfy their hunger.'

'Once they had a try on hunting living creature's flesh and digesting them freshly, this will be forever. They got addicted once they had tasted the sweetest blood ever. This is their immutable nature. I tried to warn anyone I saw on the street as if I could, so that they would watch over the mutant creatures.'

My eyes were losing sight again. Kasani held my fearful hands. 'I talked to my friend as to the evacuation two days ago. It was before the telecommunication cables were damaged severely because of this weather last night. Our government people had tried their best to fix it all up.'

'Nevertheless, I think it is just a waste of time even if they had tried the de-icing work on the road for people to travel safely. They could not fix the condition in the valley. They don't even know the existence of killing opportunity they created. Most beasts are trapped here as it is difficult for them to go far.'

'So, I have figured this out, it is no longer safe here. We have to move to somewhere rural in all these beasts' mean. I had contacted my friend previously who has been living in Batu Ferringi. It is a lot safer there as it is near the sea side.'

'Although it may not be the safest place due to its geographical factor, this may also be the prior reason that the beasts do not really like to appear in that area whereas the beasts may not be at a stronger position if they attack us there. Furthermore, it is not easy for them to travel in this depth of snow.'

'My friend told me there is an evacuee shelter centre there. Not much people there as most people had died out of the frosty weather......' When I thought he was going to continue saying, he was tearing in his soul which I heard. I wondered that was I the only person who heard voices.

7 Not compliance but only corporation

While I was thinking hard about the unknown feeling captured inside him, on the other hand, I strongly stood on my ground to unwillingly obey what he said, by saying, 'I am so sorry to say this but I really have to go and find my grandma. I can't just leave her without actually going to search for her.'

Lucas seemed so frustrated about me, and he just turned his back on me to refuse further saying anything.

At the same time, Kasani was begging me not to be rebellious at this time. Due to the ground that I would only endanger myself as if I did not want to follow what he said. As she thought he seems way tougher than we do. She added to say, I would also not be able to save my grandma whereas me myself had almost zero surviving opportunity.

Kasani expressly told me while pulling me to the awning window there which is hinged from the top as same as the one in Lucas's house. She opened slightly of the window as she wished to show me about what the reality is right now. Only the beasts were running around as if they were hunting for foods. There was not just one, but many of them.

She told me her wish to find back what she missed out but she has to first survive in order a successful eye confrontation. She explained that the persons we wished to meet, might be allocated in the refugee camp; I would have missed the precious chance to meet her if I decide to go by my own as the chance of surviving is knowingly little.

The alien seemed to understand the realistic obstacle. My head was down. So, I unwittingly agreed to stay with them to go find his friend who is staying in Batu Ferringi area right now.

Lucas looked a little bit relief now, as his eyebrows were not frowned as badly as I saw just now. Lucas said to Kasani that it is too dangerous to go out now. He recommended us to stay overnight in this garbage collecting room as the odour of the rubbish would preclude them from detecting fresh flesh.

8 Lose yourself in the cloud tonight

After that, he just provided us one sweet each person for withstanding the yearning of hunger. He then went to the other side of the room and sat there for the whole day without saying anything at all. Kasani seemed to be a little exhausted, so she just slept after she took her medicine. I knew I could never leave here even though it was dangerous outside as it would only be another dead end by staying at where we stood.

The day was too long for me to fall asleep. I rather spent my time on day-dreaming than falling asleep. Therefore, I rewound back the memory about the electrifying moment, I wondered whether he felt the same or not. I could not figure this out, but I was also demoralized to ask him personally about this.

So, I could only stare at him while thinking as to this enchanting myth. However, I noticed that every time he turned around to look towards my direction, but it would end when he saw my wide-eyed gaze. Those moisturizing eyeballs would just turn to other direction to look other way while his head stayed still.

I really felt this was funny, to the extent that I could not hold myself back and laugh by myself.

Finally, after a long wait, the night finally comes. I really could not sleep at this time mainly because of the smell in this room but still I have to endure. I have lost my sleep in the middle of the night. So again.. The only thing can accompany me now is my diary while I look at those two who sleep so comfortably under an unpleasant circumstance.

THE ADVENTURE STARTS FROM WHERE WE STOPPED

3/5/2003

1 The rise of the son of god

As I could not sleep at this time, I just got up from where I sat mutely, so that I would not wake them up. It was embarrassing to say that I could tell that Kasani and Lucas were sleeping so well even the air here was kind of polluting. I really did not understand how they did it. Anyhow, I just wanted to have a taste of fresh air.

Therefore, I decided to take a walk outside. I faintly opened the door; I did not open completely but only the space that was enough for me to go out. Before I actually laid my feet outside, I first peeped to see whether it was safe for me to go outside. I could not see anything at all. After I reassured it was entirely safe, I went out. I closed the door up immediately.

I stood in front of the door for some times as I did not know which way to go. The garbage room was right beside the stairway. I was wondering should I go up or down. I surely would never be able to feel a single blow of fresh air if I went up. Hence, I made up my mind to go down the stair.

I walked down gently and got my eyes opened fully to make sure that I could respond instantly if anything went wrong. Finally, I had reached the ground floor, I was so happy like the blossomed sunflower in the winter. It seemed a little bit different today. The street was specially clean tonight. The air was slightly warmer.

The snow I stepped on was getting watery. It was melting. I was too excited about this groundbreaking news. I started jumping up and down but I fell on the floor due to the fact that the water on the slippery floor. I got giddy at this moment. When I looked up to the sky, I saw the sky was getting brighter and it was like the sunrise was coming soon.

Suddenly, I saw a dog, it was the Lancashire. Its ear stood up, the head which got a thin, short scar on its left eye, had leaned forward, the hackles raised, and the blood near its mouth was dripping on my face. 'Wasn't that it was already dead??' I was totally freaked out. I just closed my eyes and hoped for a miracle, that Lucas would appear to save me again……

Someone was calling my name, 'Angela…. Angela….' I was thinking 'Oh…. It is Lucas….' I quickly opened my eyes, 'It's him, Lucas.' I held his hand so tight. He was asking me that, 'Are you okay?? Why are you screaming while you are sleeping??' I exhaled a long breath.

I looked around, and only realised I was still in the garbage room. What I saw just now was merely a dream. It was unfortunately lucky for me. Lucas asked me to slow down my voice if I did not want to summon 'them'. I looked at the sky through the window. I saw the newly sunrise that painted the sky in golden yellow while the sun was looking like the egg yolk I loved having as my breakfast.

The street was my first disappointment of the day. It was not like what I saw in my dream. I guess it would only be existing like a bubble, where it would end up bursting like a tragedy of the road accident that took my parents' lives. I felt the tears were accumulating in my eyes. However, I held it in like how I swallowed the pain of yesterday.

Lucas said it would be easier for us to travel during daytime while we could see things unambiguously. Lucas had become our leader. He led us down the stair like how I walked down to the stairway yesterday though it was not real. Every step we took was rigorous as we would not want to put our life at bloody risk.

When we reached the outer part of the building, the snow accumulating so high. It was like the exit had been blocked partly. Kasani and I were shivering because of the cold freezing air. The condition today was getting worse than yesterday as I could observe the difference of the depth of the snow on the ground. The depth of the snow almost reached my knee.

It really made us very difficult to walk by feet. However, by looking at the bright side of this double –edged sword, it would also make 'them' harder to haunt as well. Lucas was also telling us the same thing. I just thought whether if two persons were made for each other on this reason. There is how couples do, right?

Nevertheless, he seemed as cold as much of the ice-flake falling on my palm. It was really a mind catchy complication for me to handle. I just thought I should ignore this and concentrate on the surrounding to take caution as to the attack by the beasts. While we were walking for few hours, we never sweated under the sun as the weather was too cold for us to feel hot.

We were walking in the North direction as we were heading to Batu Ferringhi. I knew it was so far away from Lucas's house, I guess it was one of the reasons why I thought the journey seemed to be endless. I noticed something strange about Lucas. It was not the first time he shuddered. I started to feel perturbation. After a long walk, we finally found a grocery shop which was perfectly good in condition, right across the street.

Lucas suggested to us that we should take a rest first before continuing our treacherous journey. Kasani and I were saying yes with no intention to hesitate at the same time. We went nearer to the shop and only noticed it was locked up with a padlock. I knew it was wrong to appropriate stuffs which were not belonging to me but the circumstances could change though the principle of integrity was immutable.

We really got to go into the shop to get something to eat before we all fell apart because of hunger. We would not even have strength to fight against 'them'. Lucas abruptly took the thin long pin on Kasani's hair to unlock the padlock. Surprisingly, he made it. I was really impressed that this boy was omniscient as he was like a genius. He knows music, martial art… To be exact, he is good in his physical strength, and he even knows how to unlock a padlock without the key. On the other hand, this could also be the key to delinquency.

I was thinking that whether that was really a talent in the first place by reason of its incriminating nature while he opened up the door to let us in. Once the door was opened, the snow collapsed like a landslides, and even fell into the shop. We quickly closed the door and found something humongous like a steel made table to block the door.

I then sat on the floor with my hand touching the ground. It was so biting cold. It made me felt uneasy. I rapidly moved my hand away from the floor soon after I touched the mosaic floor. There was no air warmer here. I knew it would never be as comfortable as the time I was still at the hospital back then. For a sudden, I knew I missed it a lot and wondered on how people there were doing. 'Have they moved from the dying island?' 'Will our house be damaged as well? Where grandma would be right now?'

At this time, Kasani was taking a bottle of processed milk to Lucas and Lucas just took and drunk. He looked like swallowing than drinking. I could tell there was an uncommon attach by her soul from the shining eyes looking at him. As I knew how was it like, when the seed of love started to grow, it all begun with butterfly feeling and then it developed into something more than just friends after some pestering and nourishing.

It would become irreplaceable over time as its root became more concrete, and it would be impossible to remove even when you wished to. I don't know about her but this is the way how I described the formation of love.... I could actually feel the jealousy had started to grow in my heart as well when I saw other girl was in the vicinity of Lucas.

I could not just stop him from getting together with other girl even if he did not feel the same. I knew it was so wrong to own this feeling inside so I wished to wither it away. However, it was too tough for me to win over this battle. I really hated myself to have too much conflict during this time.

Lucas did not seem to fulfil his hunger. He went all over the store to search, but no body knew what he wanted to look for. He threw the unfavourable tins on the floor. It was abnormal. We were shocked in silence. We just continued with the consumption. As we knew any word would make up provocation.

Before we actually finished our lunch, I heard thunderbolt. It was like going to rain very soon. We all decided to stay here for the night as to avoid any forthcoming danger if we were stubborn to continue our journey. We had made a right choice, as there was an undesirable storm hitting us.

I was totally stunned when the sky turned darker as it was in this early morning. The clusters of cloud were unbelievably gigantic. The wind gusts were raging until the tree at the road side at the front of the roadway had been ripped off. Lucas knew it was going to be unpredictably hazardous. He immediately asked two of us to hide under the steel table, just in case that the roofs of this place collapsed or was hurled away.

It was not snowfall. It looked more like rainfall. It is something like freezing rain. The speed of the sustained wind had reduced the visibility of the view as the snow on the ground had whirled all over the place. In latter time, the variation was then appeared. The snow now substituted the rain. A bleak weather that kept changing......

We hoped the roof is the durable one......

As there is pale moon on the night sky tonight, it is getting darker in the shop. I have made use of the weak sun beam that I can get through the transparent glass of the door to record what I saw today whereas Kasani is too tired to stay alert after she has taken her prescribed medication. Only...... Lucas just stared at the monstrous phenomena.

I noticed 'The colour of his ferocious eyes is changing!' I knew it was never a good news. I approached him, 'Hi Lucas. How are you doing today? I found first aid equipment, I can help you to disinfect all over again the accidental wound.' He turned his eyes to my direction. His eyes, those brownish red. This was not I originally remembered. He shuddered again. He held his wound and answered, 'Don't worry. I am fine.'

This looks really horrific. He refused for me to help him. It is hurt to hear that but should I think his words are reliable? However, in the back of mind, I keep thinking back the myth of 'The lucky star' lately, that I really hope all the inauspicious moment will be perished right away.

A POTENTIAL SAVIOUR

<u>4/5/2003</u>

1 The continuance

The weather has been made no difference today though the wind did not seem to be as strong as yesterday but the snowfall was quite heavy. The snow accumulating outside the door of the shop, is getting amazingly higher than what I saw yesterday. I have tried to compare the height of the elevating snow with the length of my legs. It almost achieved the height of my chest.

As you know anxiety is haunting endlessly while I am thinking that 'Would we be trapping here like forever and ever?? Is this the end of the journey??' I have been thinking about these question so oftenly. As I thought I would die with greatest regret on the ground that, grandma would be remained unknown like forever. There are too much of uncertainty. I wonder how to cope.

I don't know about the fact where may survival be available under the merciless whipping of the coldness in this unwelcoming winter, whereas I am just thinking about the feasible chance. Whether I should have confessed what I have towards the one who saved me from the bloody mouth? Looking at those eyes. It is snowballing but it attracts me the most.

I know for sure about the possibility for redressing the mistake I made, is not really bright. I can't even guarantee that I would be able to go to the refugee camps alive or not. Despite the dream, grandma might have waited for me there. The only thing I have full control of my discretion is to cherish what I have.

I always feel like we share the same feeling too especially after reading this diary. At the same time, the curious voice keeps telling me about what if. 'What if he was the one?', 'What if we were the perfect match even before this unfortunate disaster?' However, he seemed to fall for another when grandma started to object the proposed love story.

He might be belonging to another girl now. What about Kasani?? I can see complication here.

If I step in, it would not just be a triangle issue but also seemed wrong to own others' thing for the sake of desire. As I know it would affect those innocent party, it is never my intention. Furthermore, as a gentleman, wouldn't be he making the first step to nourish the seed of love, would he?? He seems as cold as the weather here to me.

He trembles strongly day by day. He looks unusually fairer nowadays. I am really feeling hard to see him like this. I want to help him, but rejection is all he has ever given me. I am full of these annoyance. I can't subsist any longer. I want to quit the childish game but it is only a thought.

By thinking about this, I really feel mad at this stubbornness. Whenever he lays his ferocious eyes on me, I just turn my head away or look toward the wise professional man in this four wall room. Speaking of this man, he is the new member who just newly arrived at our 'indestructible' battleship today. Welcome on board!

This man looks thoroughly intelligent, he is a middle-aged man, I think.... On the basis that, he is wearing a black frame glasses with a formal dress code; such as an originally snowy white like shirt with a dusted laboratory uniform as an outer layer, as well as a long black coloured pants. With the dirt, he really looks like a down-town profession to me.

I don't know if others notice that the trouble he might get into from the past few days.

2 Someone who needed help?

As a result of the noises created by the blizzard, we woke up in this morning right after the clock hanged on the wall in this shop turned nine. We just simply took the junk foods we loved to be made as our breakfast. We were busy to help maintaining the metabolism rate of our body except for the fancy eyes.

The air here was so much warmer if compared to yesterday. I guess it might be because of the warmer air we kept breathing out, had trapped in the room that kept us warm.

Something I saw in the early morning had made me disgusted about myself. As I just felt uncomfortable when the innocent soul kept approaching the hungry mouth like a twin brother and sister. She just took him favourite drink, a canned Milo, and passed it to him. When he took the Milo from her, he accidentally touched the tips of her fingers. She immediately shrank like a shy tortoise. She held her head down with a sweet smile on her beautifully pale face.

He eventually put down the canned Milo, and expressed his thankful mind by shrugging while holding his wounded arm. It was all so tight. There must be something he tries to hide or preclude from that feebly fiercely face. As a friend or not, I really don't want to see it happen.

Lucas seemed like there was nothing happening a few minutes ago. He went to the other end of the corner to search for his breakfast. He finally found one. He grabbed a few tins. I was not sure what he was holding. All I knew was he behaved with his unruliness.

At this time, I was staring at the amazed eyes, I really wanted to give her at least one chance to pursue something she wants so badly for the very first time during lifetime. I knew she found this rare.

Nevertheless, I felt something devil whispering to my ears. It is a matter of choice. It is all depending on my indecisive nature. As I deserve to fight for what I want, moreover, it is not criminal. Life is too short for hastening. His status is so obscure. Clarification is needed so desperately.

However, back in my head, I just know its expediency is so wrong. I never wanted to ruin others' happiness. Soon after, insanity has become part of my sanity. The itchiness I wished to precluded.

The day looked totally upside down from what I perceived today. It seemed clear outside the shrouding space. However, I noticed something moving clumsily outside in spite of the uncertain conflict in me. I wished to stop thinking about the rift that would make three of us to fall apart like a broken mirror.

Therefore, I came closer to the transparent glass of the door which permitted me to see through what was going on outside. I stood in distance from the door, so that the view I had been inspecting, would not vanish due to the height of the accumulating snow.

It was a snow white man from far. He looked so giddy as he was staggering in a zigzag to our direction. There was a beast behind him. I guess it was too difficult to move on the highly elevating snow. It was moving unsteadily too but still it was just few steps away to catch its prey for dinner tonight.

Lucas responded quickly by asking us to assist him in thrusting the table to the other side, so that it would not block the doorway. In spite of the wound, he acted with powerful source. It was unorthodox! I heard someone snoring violently. It disappeared when I started to look around.

Without further consideration, we all used up all the strength to open the door by way of pulling. I think, most probably, the accumulating snow and the weather outside had incurred the intensity of air pressure outside the shop. It made up the significant difference of the content found outside and the pressure inside the shop.

While we were pulling the door handle harder, I heard something knocking the glass of the door. I looked up to find out what was the source. I saw the man was battling with the beast bare hand. He was so brave though he seemed so vulnerable. He first held the mouth with both hands so that he would not get bitten. He then kept punching the beast with his right hand until it lost consciousness.

He later thrust it to a further place. We eventually got the door opened. The snow collapsed again. He just fell on the ground from the where he originally stood. We all surrounded him like he was an alien. He looked at us and tried to get up, 'I am alright. Thank you for concerning. I am a normal man. You should see it better now.'

Kasani led him to sit at the side whereas I and Lucas tried to close the door properly before any gruesome creature would get in and attack us. I heard him coughing and muttering at the same time, 'There are too many scattering pieces of memory I can't really remember.'

Lucas went near to him, 'Are you alright, Mr ...??' I purposely said like I was an opposition, 'Of course, he is alright. Can't you see the way he hit the beast like he got super power.' I got him looking at me again.

He replied, 'I am fine, thank you for your concern and I just put on my very best effort to survive here. I just can't remember about my past ever since I woke up in the middle of the snowy land. However, the weirdness I can't explain is that I do remember about knowledge that I have been studying about snowing.' I thought to myself, 'Snow?? Could he be the one to stop all these non-sense??'

3 The 'snow' man

He started to demonstrate things happening now, 'What we see now is an event of winter storm. It is where the varieties of precipitation are formed.

It is like the process of converting water into snow. By providing that the temperatures are substantially low, it guarantees the success of the conversion. Sometimes, if the ground temperatures are low enough, it will enable ice to form things like freezing rain during rainstorm.'

I asked out of curiosity, 'Freezing rain??? I think I saw once yesterday, it made no difference with the rainfall in normal season in Malaysia.' He interrupted, 'Yes. It does but do you know that the rain drop will freeze when it falls on the ground, such as the surface of the road or anything which is heat transmittable, like steel. Therefore, the surface will undoubtedly become even more slippery than usual.'

The room was filled with soundless element. We all just stopped talking while our body were frozen like chicken in the fridge. I was really surprised about this guy that he would know so much about what we encounter now.

Despite how we responded to his words, he went on to say, 'We still have to take note even if the weather now seems a little bit relaxing. It is because it may be a blizzard. It is a weather condition involving snow but still containing variable definitions in different parts of the world.'

I could tell that he seemed so excited to give his talk. He took a long breath and then continued explaining that, 'As far as I concerned, what I said could be exemplified that, as in the United States, a blizzard occurs when the specific two conditions are met with a good timing. The worse is that the visibility can be reduced to less than 0.4 kilometers (0.25mi) by reason of frequent gusts to thirty five miles per hour (56 km/h).'

'That's not just it. It was also included sufficient snow in the air as well. It is where the criteria are more or less the same in the Western Countries like Canada and United States. When heavy snowfall often occurs during blizzard conditions, falling snow is not an actual requirement, as blowing snow can literally create a monstrous ground blizzard. We might experience the symptom of shortness of breathing as a consequence of the winter storm. So, we should never underestimate the damage this fellow could bring…'

By hearing what he said, the sense of creepy sinks in as if the day is going to end right away due to the raging weather does not seem to stop. However, I still feel glad about his appearance. On the basis that I don't know why but I just think his knowledge might be the golden key to solve this mystery. The wise locally 'snow' man……

A sincere hope is placed on the hopeless land I have been living for fourteen years. It could really turn back to the way it was before. I miss hot air that we can actually run around on the field with no fear that the blizzard weather would attack the motherland. The magic is made as the sun beats down on us.

The rainbow that touches the clear blue sky delicately whenever the rain stops. The birds always sing to perform beautifully as if they are well-trained for it. There are even pigeons in group all over the town or my house place. I may see them feed on the field though I don't know what they actually feed on.

The sun beam runs through the window to wake me up, so that I will not be late to go to school with grandma's accompany. All these things can only live in part of my recovered memory now....

THE STORY – TELLER

<u>5/5/2003</u>

1 Keep on going

We were actually got stuck for two days. Today, the third day we were in this shop. I impatiently woke up in this fresh morning as I could not really sleep last night after hearing his words. As I just wanted to get out from here as soon as possible. When I first opened eyes, it was unknowingly going uphill for me to breathe. I guess, most probably, I was having a nightmare which I could not remember.

I was caught in the state of chaos for a few minute by just staring at the floor. I looked straight to the view outside the transparent glass of the door from where I was lying, right after I regained consciousness from my day dream. I had pictures flashing in my mind. It was Lucas. He was eating after he sniffed over the food.

He sniffed before he ate! I must have been mistaken. This is not how to be categorized in our level! I must have been thinking about him so frequently. I can't trust my eyes sometimes. Kasani was pointing her tender bone at the scene outside. I then followed. The sky was clearly azure with clusters of white cloud until the sun was invisible because of that reason. It was brightening blue you have ever seen since that day. It just looked exactly like the day I received this diary as a gift from grandma.

I was thinking that, 'Could it be a good sign for us by indicating that it was a striking hope to overturn this heart-thrilling fallout??' The 'snow man' suddenly shouted, 'Allah, thank you for granting my wish upon my pray.' whereas Lucas stood up energetically, and said, 'Finally, we waited so long for this day to come, these two days were like waiting to go for the execution of hanging to death. One minute is like spending ten years here.'

After finishing up our breakfast, we started to move the steel table aside together, and then pulled the handle of the door to open. I guess it was too hard to open. We had consumed all the strength we just preserved for ten minutes. Lucas was extremely fervent as he looked healthier than anyone of us here. I wondered why those eyes were vanished.

We continued to push, and eventually the door was opened but four of us just fell on the ground while the accumulating snow fell on us as how it all collapsed. It was icy cold. I did shiver.

Nonetheless, I think it was so fun for me to play with the snow during this difficult time. At least, it is not a sour odyssey to me. I kept giggling when Kasani tried to throw some snow at me and at the same time, I did the same to her. We were happily playing in the snow like I did not remember the ruling jealousy I had for the past two days.

2 A brand new day

I guess it was the time. A good time to let go of the hopeless confusion. Lucas took his knife and torchlight while three of us just took what we needed for our lunch. When we stepped out of the shop, the ground was like slithery than the previous time because of the great quantities of the snow.

However, we were still able to get out from the small cliff. I was exhaling a deep, long breath. I did not know why. A feeling crept in. I just thought like as if I was just released from imprisonment. I felt so good about everything as if I forgot as to the existence of the beast. Lucas asked me to slow down my voice unless I wanted to become their lunch later.

We had been walking around but it was revolving the same spot. We could not really recognise the buildings and the roads along the way as all of them looked the same to us. Most of the buildings were damaged severely. The reason why we would not know what the building originally was, whereas the roads were snowy as the coverage of the snow was substantially great. Everything was in white; the road signs were also remained unfound like it never existed.

We went round and round but we still came back to the store where we were staying for two days. We got lost in this white land. We tried to put a mark on every damaged house we walked by, just to make sure we would not go through the same way. While we were walking, I heard some noises behind us. My instinct told me something. It was watching over us.

3 Who's at my back?

When I looked back, I did not find anyone or anything tailing our back. By spending a few hours in searching a correct way, we finally had our fruit of harvest. We saw a partially damaged road sign right beside the Genegles Hospital. The sign board was dented in the center; as a result, we could not see properly what was written on the board.

Therefore, we went closer to check it out. Everything we did. We would stick together to deter the 'unwanted friend' to visit. As we knew, they would unlikely be attacking human in group due to their unsecured position. Debilitates their plan of attacking. I saw the words 'Batu Ferringhi' at the last two row there and according to the road sign, there were still fifty kilometres away to reach our destination.

At this time, I just looked up to the sky to see. I prayed for it to be appropriate for a continuation to walk. The sky looked a little greyish than what we saw in the morning. The sun was still remaining invisible until now. There was only deadly sound in the sky as opposed to what I had seen for the past two months. I could not even see a fly flying around in this horrific winter.

The tree I saw right beside the main entrance to the Genegles Hospital. It had already started fraying like a piece of silk as it had lost all of its leaves, the branches were partly hurled. The roots had become visible due to the fact it had slanted like it was going to collapse soon.

There was a truck locating at more than ten steps away from us. It should match the likely estimation. It seemed like it was abandoned as it looked white by reason of snow covering the whole body, while it got no one sitting on the driver seat. I could actually recognise this kind of truck. It had been used for purpose of de-icing.

Lucas went towards that direction to investigate. The rest of us just followed what he did. We saw blood stain on the driver seat. Lucas put his hand on the driver seat to touch to rub the blood stain. He sniffed and then said, 'The blood stain was dry in spite of the cold weather might affect the consumption of time for blood to clot.

It could be speculated that the truck had already been left for few days according to the accumulation of the snow on the truck itself. Well, by remembering what he said, I feel spooky. I just dislike the feeling of nothing like pizzazz that lives would provide. Everything seemed so dull in a mortal city.

I still had the feeling of being watched even if I saw no one following us. While I tried to express what I felt, Lucas said, 'hey, guys. I thought it was better for us to stay overnight here. The weather seems to be unforeseeable; furthermore, we are not alone in this frozen city.'

I got his eyes on me for only one second. It was a satisfaction. Lucas continued, 'I am not sure whether we can find a place for us to rest in further part. I am also worried about the weather. I think we should stay overnight in the hospital unless we could find a better choice. How about this? Guys??'

The snow man just kept quiet there unlike his talkative character I observed yesterday while Kasani smiled at Lucas and said delicately, 'Okay, whatever you say, I will just follow.' Lucas then stared at me, I could see the wait without patience. I just answered, 'Whatever it is, I follow the majority.' Lucas raised his eyebrow and then only said, 'Okay, great. Come on everyone, let go in.'

I guess he never took the snow man in consideration. On the ground that his personal opinion was not in the list of concerning, but I wondered why. I still went into the hospital in spite of thinking about the ambiguity. While we were walking by a guard house, we saw the door closed improperly.

We never thought that much. We just walked into the hallway. The surrounding was quite dark as the sunlight was too dim to illuminate the whole place while the electric supply had been cut off. I could see no one here. I imagined that people here must have been running away once they heard about the attack of dogs in this area.

Suddenly, I heard some noises from our back. Kasani screamed so loud at my back. I freaked out. We all then turned our heads around. It was surprising. The elevators here were still working. 'It could be the spare electric generator.' The snow man said.

Lucas suggested to go to fifth floor of this building which was also the highest floor in here, he managed to justify it. What was heard was that the beasts would not be accessing to us easily as if we made sure the elevators and stairways were adequately blocked to preclude them.

We all did what he said. We carefully observed the environment and made sure there was no existence of potential danger. We went to fifth floor by way of elevators and then we used a few long wooden cubes to prevent all the elevators in this particular floor to work or to close their doors in that floor. Surprisingly, to me, I never knew elevators could still be functioning even if there was no electric supply. It was scary but I guess he was right. They might have operated through the preserved energy supply that was normally found in commercial building.

Nevertheless, it was not nothing more than just terrifying.

We also locked the door of the stairways by using the padlock we found on the door of the stairways itself. Having done all the precautions we could actually think of, I realised the sky was getting darker. The night was going to take over. We all went into a private ward which was a single – bed room. We blocked the door by pushing the bed to the door like how we did in the grocery shop.

We all just sat on the floor and rest with our eyes opened wide. I heard it groaning. It might be a complaint but there was nothing else I could do. I sat right opposite the window which allowed me to look out of the street or even the sky before I could fall asleep.

I felt a little warmer. I thought others might need it. So, I just took off my jackets and asked the snow man whether he needed it or not. He just rejected my offer politely even though he looked kind of depressed today. A sad voice was heard, 'It is ok, thanks. I don't feel cold at all. Furthermore, you are so much thinner than I do. I think you need the jackets more than I actually do.'

4 The untold one is remained untold

I smiled at him and took the courage to ask, 'I have been calling you the snow man. What is your real name? Do you remember??'

He answered, 'Yea, I do. My name is Samsur. I remember that I have a daughter but I forgot about her name and even my wife's name.'

I felt sympathy towards his loss of memory as I knew how exactly it felt like. I wished to comfort him by patting his shoulder but right before I did, he started talking again, 'I remember my daughter. She is so adorable, as she seemed like a Barbie doll to me. As she got her mother eyes, big and round while it looks a little watery.'

He said he also remembered when his wife wanted to give birth to her at the hospital. The moment of rushing to the hospital just because he wanted to be right beside her while she needed him the most. However, it fell out of the expectation. He just stopped telling his story and fell asleep just like that.

'What does he mean in his words? He could not make it, couldn't??' I hoped to know more but he just slept so comfortably, I just thought it was better not to wake him up. I then looked out of the window. I saw a very bright halo in the sky like a giant spotlight shinning on me.

I remember the science astrology project during primary school time. I did the research myself. That's why it stuck here. It is an intriguing science fact. The halo is a type of ring. It always surrounds the moon or even the sun in specific circumstances.

The conditions of construction may be the refraction of light with a thin cloud of ice crystals. We can find red colours inside of the halo ring shifting to blue on the outside. It looks exactly as in the explanation of the research. I was used to know about this phenomena by theory. I never thought I could actually witness it with my own eyes....

'Should I say it is glad to see the grant of gem?'

I really don't know what else's going to happen next. Thinking about the blinded future, I feel anxiety rolling wild in me. I wish to fall asleep as easy as them but I can't. Lucas is sleeping right beside Kasani while her head is leaning on his shoulder.... By watching them, I just feel nonchalant.

At this kind of moment, I literally confuse about myself.

THE BEAUTIFUL WOUND
THAT SLITS MY HEART

<u>6/5/2003</u>

1 The beautiful scene causes the wide-eyed gaze

As I could not sleep well at all, I opened my eyes and looked around. I was pretty sure I was not dreaming this time. Mr. Samsur was sleeping while the wrinkled lips kept murmuring. I did not even know what was he talking, even if I tried to listen by leaning closer to his direction.

I then looked straight to Lucas and Kasani. Two of them were still closing their eyes and the sleepy head on his shoulder. They looked exactly like a newly sweet couple together. If this would be our future, I would still feel happy for their unity. I guess the time was still very early, and thus, as usual, I sat on the floor while leaving my eyes vacant.

The sky was still dark in the earlier time whereas I could not see anything in the sky. There was no moon, stars, or even clouds. However, a wish was granted. I later saw something miraculous. It was beautifully stunning, I just could not take my eyes of 'you'. The sun pillars I saw during the sunrise. It was so eye pleasing as it was something I never seen before in my whole life.

As I always preferred indoor activities, I never really appreciated the chance of getting kissed by the sun's rays while I was still enabled to enjoy it. Nowadays, it is weird to see that I only started to grow my love to the Mother Nature when not many chances are left. However, a representative of a new fondly hope in the starry eyed sight. I was going to start the day by watching the natural supernatural on the basis that it was only happening in the winter which Malaysia did not normally have.

It was where the luminous vertical streaks of light. They were slightly painted reddish in colour. I saw them expanding from above and below the sun. They seemed more like a reflection due to the mirror effect to me. I think, most likely, it was because of the surface of the ice crystal containing in the clouds that constituted the cause of the phenomenal scientific norm.

In later time, I then saw the crepuscular rays among the clouds. It was like the clouds were planning up to preclude the sun from lightening up the surface of the earth but the evil never won. The bands of horizontal sunlight were shining through the gaps. Looking at those clouds. It made me realised that every cloud has a silver lining. A motivation relieves the horrified bubble hope.

I wished I could freeze this beautiful scene but unfortunately, I did not have a camera with me. Well, it is okay because everything I saw would be captured in my mind without her. 'I will remember it.' I told myself. I guess the bright sunlight was too annoyed for Mr. Samsur to continue his lovely dream. He was awakened by the call of the new day.

2 Who's that?

The weather here was extremely perfect for us to travel. After Lucas and Kasani woke up, we all agreed to move on. When we came out from the room, the dark shadows passed by to the stairway. On the way, I saw a feathery thick jacket on the floor. I guess it was too dark yesterday for me to notice it.

I picked it up and handed over to Mr. Samsur, 'Mr. Samsur, I think it is better to wear this because I worry if you would catch cold by just wearing this shirt.' He took the jacket from me and said, 'Thanks… You remind me of my daughter. She should be at your age by now.'

I just smiled at him and then the wordless conversation. While I turned my head to the front, Lucas was also doing the same thing! I felt wondered that 'Was he peeping on me?', but whatever is it, it was not the matter anymore. Before we actually walked out from the same door that we came in yesterday, we heard the calls from our hunger again.

Lucas spotted a mini-market in the hospital itself, at the opposite end of the front door. We followed him to search for foods. While I was walking, the feeling of being watched haunted me again. I just felt that there was someone else here in spite of four of us. I walked too feebly until Lucas called my name so loudly from the mini-market. 'Hey, Angela, I got your favourite green tea over here. Hurry up.'

I tried to walk faster when I started to realise I was alone in the middle of the walk path. I later ran to their direction. Suddenly, I saw the door of a staff room opened partly. I was too afraid to respond at this time, I just stood with my legs shaking tremendously. The door was opened widely, and a boy walking out of the room was leaning to me, I could not support his weight, so we fell on the floor.

We were stacking up. By looking at his face, I had forgotten about the pain I felt momentarily. With his flawless complexion, I guess he should be at around my age. He took a glance at me before he got fainted with his right hand pressing his left ribs. I could really feel his heart was beating like my breath at this moment. They were so consistent. At the same time, I could feel my right hand become watery. I took up to see, 'It is blood. He is wounded.'

3 Humanitarian always win

Lucas and the rest came up and helped. Lucas and Mr. Samsur held him up and check out his wound. Kasani just helped me out by holding me up from where I fell. It appeared again. He shivered by holding on his wound on the right arm. I wondered, 'It's still not recovering?' Those fiercely eyes were back!

Mr. Samsur said his wound was not quite serious, just that the loss of substantive blood had made his live at stake.

I and Kasani went up to the room where the necessary medical equipment for the purpose of treating the boy could be found. A hope to prevent further bleeding. Mr. Samsur and Lucas carried him back to the room where we were staying last night and Mr. Samsur then went out to find antibiotic for the boy as he started to have fever.

I thought. Based on what I speculated from his proficiency in medical knowledge, Mr. Samsur might be a doctor before he passed out and forgot everything. It was not within our expectation. Me and Kasani heard people fighting on the stairway. We ran back immediately to the room. Mr. Samsur tried to hold Lucas on the floor. Lucas was immobile.

Mr. Samsur screamed, 'Hurry! He needs to be anaesthesia!!! Faster!! I can't hold him any longer!!' I ran to the other room to look for what had been told. I ransacked all the drawers in the pharmacy room. I could not find it! At this critical moment, I froze and then heard Kasani screaming, 'Please don't hurt him!'

I closed my pressured eyes and started to think where else to find the weakening medicine. I was concentrating but the on-going battle. I went to a malfunctioned fridge. It was summoning me. I opened up. Finally, I grabbed and ran back to the menacing scene. Lucas was opening his bloody mouth wide. He was ready to start dining on Mr. Samsur.

It was terrified! Kasani was scared and hid at the back of the bed found in the room. I ran to the front. I got my hand held high and penetrated the bloody veined skin with anaesthetic. We broke as we heard the shriek of woe. He turned his back on his potential dinner. He looked at me. The fiercely eyes started to get falling off. He put his violent hand on my right shoulder. He recognised me! The hug we had before he passed out.

Mr. Samsur asked, 'Are you hurt?' 'No.' I panted heavily. 'You?' Mr. Samsur grinned, 'I am fine! No wound made by him so far.' 'What happened? Why he attacked you so suddenly?' Mr. Samsur explained, 'No idea, it was when we carried the one on the floor back into the room. He gave me the hungry look. He started to push me away and prey on the boy. He began with licking the fresh blood dripping down the floor!'

I was shocked! The part of the beast intruded his purest soul. I should have known? He turned into a monster because of me? The weirdness I should have speculated earlier!! I tried to hold on my tears but failed. Mr. Samsur continued, 'I fought with him to make sure no body get hurt.' I quickly took off his jacket to strip the long sleeve shirt on the veined skin.

The wound was exacerbating. It never got better. I elucidated as Mr. Samsur questioned. He tried to examine and went to grab some medicine for these two feeble hearts. I speculated the trigger of his barbarity was the fresh blood. We found a long strip of clothes. I was sorry but we decided to tide him up for the sake of safety.

Nobody in this time knows how to cure this kind of zombified disease. Mr. Samsur was trying to fix this issue. It was a horrible scene. He removed the putridity. He put those unauthorised antibiotic into the mutated mouth.

I heard the teardrops on the cool ground later. I was too worried about this boy too, so I just stayed right beside him, just in case he might need my assistance as if he woke up.

After the incident, we all thought staying overnight would be the best selection for now.

We can't just turn around and walk off. These was not we originally planned. It was dangerous and hazardous but we would not want to leave them behind. I hope this will change when I wake up in the next morning. The sweet humanity during the irregular difficult time I felt tonight. It was like the heart-warming fire sparkles found in the snowy land.

I pray hard for these boys to survive tonight, I do not know why I feel that much. A wish for him to stay alive. Here I am again tonight. I am wide awake. So, I just spend my time by writing my diary.

THE RACE WITH TIME STARTS NOW

7/5/2003

1 Rift that drives him crazy

I guess I was too tired yesterday. I fell asleep just like that without I realised it. When I opened my eyes, I was still holding this diary in my hand. At the same time, my head was laying on the boy's chest. I would not have waked up if I was not shocked nearly to death.

While I was sleeping, there was a person patting my right shoulder so hard. I turned my head around with the loudly beating sound. My eyebrows frowned when his eyes were having no distance with mine. He managed to loosen the deadly tight tie. 'I am hungry. What's happened yesterday? I realise I was tied up when I woke up today.'

My breath started to get heavy. It was the noise you could hear in silence. I then observed while my legs were squirming backward. The veined skin seemed normal as how we all have. The fiercely eyes were tamed. He breathed like the sleeping beauty. He asked me as if I was sick.

'Can I see your wound?' I asked with the borrowed courage. He said, 'Surprisingly, it was not that disturbing as last time anymore.' He then showed me his expected arm. I was stunned. The wound was healed overnight with a fresh new scar. It was unbelievable! He was also giving me an astonishing look. I told him what he did yesterday. He was scratching his head with a replay button.

He could not recall at all. He continued to say, 'Never mind. It does not bother me as much as this!' The anguish air was breathed out. I felt it. He then looked at the boy. He just walked off like that with no word added to this early morning conversation. I am glad he is back but it was getting worse. I mean......

He seemed a little bit moody today like the weather I saw in this morning. It was like a bad news for a good news. He did not even have a smile on his face like I was doing wrong to him. He held me up and said, 'It's okay. You can leave the boy alone now. I am pretty sure that he has gone through the dangerous state. All we have to do is to wait for him to wake up.'

He then thrust me to the other direction. I almost fell, but luckily the awakened Mr. Samsur held me up. He then said, 'Are you okay?? His condition is getting sad.' I quickly explained what I saw this morning. We were whispering while Lucas did not really want to give any attention, and then he walked away like that. I was struggling in a turbulent space as I just could not figure out the reason why I had to be treated in that way.

I felt heartbroken out of the relieving trepidation. I was really angry at that moment. I just went to the corner and sat there. My heart was beating like rhythms in the frustrated mind. I just sat at the corner there to allocate the messy pieces of melody in proper order, while he went out together with the cheerful girl, to bring some foods back to us.

<u>Funny thing</u>
when we first met, it is only days
Everything seemed so fine
You're being so nice

I caught you turned your head away
When my eyes were on you
You're just like a little boy
And I see......
We don't usually speak
I feel strange every time we do.
And it happened again.

Oh~~~ oh~~~~
I just said
This is a funny thing
It will happen like an appointment made
I really don't understand
How it has to be the same.

Should not I call it?
Lucky but elegiac.
Though it is hurt than I ever thought
But I still wanna be different this time.

So, do you have to be that funny?
Funny? Funny? Funny?
Will you do me a favour?
Will you? Will you? Will you??

2 It was spring time in my heart

It tore me in pieces; I started crying even though I did not want to. Mr Samsur, who was sitting beside me, not to say that he tried to unbreak my heart, but relieve my pain that I felt deeply inside. I still wonder why. At this moment, we heard someone's coughing in debilitation. I opened my blood-shot eyes completely. I looked around and found out that the boy was awake.

I ran to his direction in just a minute. I leaned to him. He kept blinking his vacant eyes delicately. I took a bottle of an unopened mineral water to him in order to let him sipping. However, he drank the water like there was something devil pulling him inward which made him gorged.

I asked him to slow down but he seemed like he was having impaired of hearing. After finished one whole bottle of water, he laid down on the floor. He looked more responsive than the earlier time. He asked with his clueless facial expression, 'Where am I?'. I replied delightful, 'You are at where you were. You are still at the hospital. Remember?? You fell on me before you passed out.'

He frowned his eyebrows. He was trying to think harder with strenuous effort about what I said. He then kept quiet innocently. I happily smiled at him, and answered, 'It's okay if you cannot remember. Let me elucidate in detail. I do not know when you got into this hospital… We just got here two days ago. I only found you yesterday morning before we actually left this place.'

'When we found you, you were already injured. The wound on your left ribs was not serious. Just that you lost blood severely. I can tell you are recovering speedily.'

He looked at me with staunch eye-sight like he had figured out something. His fascinating eyes had caught you in the state of whimsy. It made me lost my sensibility. It was like the application of magic spell on me. The spell was so violently strong, I could never break it by myself. I was asking myself, 'Is this real?'.

His eyes were fluttering as if he was searching for something, he then looked at me, 'I remember something that I want to tell, but it is so bleary. I can't recall.' He closed his eyes tightly for a few second. He then opened it again so suddenly. He exhaled a long breath.

He held my wrist up gently tight and said, 'I remember you, the girl who has curly, short hair. I saw you before. Somewhere ….' I replied, 'Really??' 'Would he be the one who had been tailing us all the way to this hospital according to an intuitive sense?' I thought to myself.

3 The insanity went wild??

Lucas came back at this time. Lucas pulled my hand off the boy's hand. I was shocked unexpectedly. It will never end. It was the second time. I guess the boy was having the same commotion as well. Two of us were looking at each other with question marks flying all over our brains. Lucas yelled at me again, 'You better stay at where you are now. Do you think it is the best time to play the love game??'

I was really curious to know, 'He is still sick?'. The way he clung on my hand was hurtful. I was requesting him to let go of my hand. He seemed like he was too mad to listen to what I said. Kasani, who was standing beside him, tried to persuade him on fulfilling my quest. Mr. Samsur knew something went wrong. He came up to Lucas to calm him down in order to get his hand off me.

Lucas then looked into my eyes with affirmative expression. I was assured that he got something to tell me, but he did not want to. 'What is it??' My heart was asking. He wished to tell me something but he just stayed silent instead. Why I always feel he is someone that I am familiar with?? However, I am not meant to fall for a triangle gossip while the story seems so hopeless and, what about her??' I thought by myself.

At this moment, the boy suddenly shouted so loudly, 'I know who you are.' I was thinking that he knew who I was, 'Seriously??' However, I had no sign of remembering his charming face.

4 The past is not the matter now

With the adorably innocent face, he got up though he seemed giddy. I wished to help but my movement was absolutely restricted by his tubby hand. I was disabled to go further away from Lucas. The boy came closer while Lucas kept leaning backward. It should be the other way round but he turned it all over. He stopped moving, and he then put his knee down.

He started to cry with regretful grief, 'I am so sorry, I should be responsible for what I have done but I am too afraid of admitting my wrongdoing that I just ran away from my culpability.'

Scratching my scalp should stop someday. 'I am so glad that you are still alive. I have been tortured by my hidden conscience every single night. I found out as to your news in newspaper. I did try to confess my wrong officially but, at the same time, I was struggling with the conflicting facts between the ingrained guilt and selfishness inside me. I know I do not deserve of getting your renegade forgiveness though I wish to…..'

Having heard what he claimed, I recalled back what Fazlim said about 'hit and run case'. I thought, 'Is he talking about this pathetic memory of mine?' Lucas started to let go of my hand and I just pulled my hand away from him. I went a few paces forward to the boy, and asked unfaithfully, 'Are you the one who drove the lorry and knocked me down, then drove away with ignorance??'

He answered with his shaky voice, 'Yes… I was the one. I would just say, I am sorry for a million times if you wanted me to do so.' The room was immediately filled with unpleasantly concealing thought. I was literally paralysed by this confusing interruption. The one I thought he was hopeful, was a merely misunderstanding.

I was really curious about the justification for his negligence. So, I asked aggressively like No tolerance for escape from answering my invisibly questionnaires in mind. He seemed like he was obliged to provide me a satisfying genuine answer to all question marks put to him. He was reminded of five months ago where he got chased out of his house because of being a badly truant. He later stole the keys to the lorry of his father's belonging, and drove even though he had no licence at all.

He thought it would be as easy as how he watched his father did. He just thought of somewhere to release out the frustration by driving his father's lorry. He eventually lost of control on the lorry by reason of speeding and inadvertently hit on the one who was walking alone on the pavement. He did stop the lorry forcefully to save me, but he changed his mind after the next minute he stopped the lorry. He just drove away like that.

I guess I was wrong about him. The magical confrontation was broken as much as I found out that he, who was the associative culprit of the tragedy. Due to his moral culpability and the irresponsibility, the reliability was essentially ravaged. I was being notified of his conscience.

At last, the conscience still wins. He might be in whole again. However, I was thinking in the back of my mind that what would I get if I kept blaming him for the same mistake. Nothing could be undone. I could never rewind back to the time I started losing people I love. I could neither save my long hair from being shaved, nor it could bring us to the destination safely.

I spoke to him, 'What past is past. It does not matter now. What is at stake is we can get to the evacuation centre at Batu Ferringhi in complete.' The boy said, 'Do you mean the evacuation centre in Rasa Sayang Hotel at Batu Ferringhi??' Mr. Samsur finally started to speak, 'You know about that evacuation centre??? How??'

Mr. Samsur seemed so desperate to know more as to that centre, even though we told him before as to the basic information we knew from Lucas. The beautifully tearing eyes replied, 'Yes. Of course, I do. I was there before I got here. I originally followed the crowd to the evacuation centre but not my father. It was because I have not gone back home for months since he chased me out of his house. I could not find him in the centre. I was so worried about him so I went back secretly to his house to search for him.'

He shook his head delicately, 'Furthermore, the specially made boarding ship Indonesia; they are going to send here is arriving soon; sending us out from this country will depend; before it all comes to an end. I really wish to go with my father. At the time, I got back home, the house was already collapsed. I tried to find out whether my father was buried in the snow, but the weather was too harsh for me to continue. Later on, the dogs in group were attacking me.'

He exhaled, 'I was lucky. I escaped from them successfully though I got injured when running away from them like crazy. I then saw her walking with you guys, I could really recognise her though her hair looked much shorter, if compared to the time I saw her during the accident. I followed you guys at the back there though I felt weaker every steps I walked. I thought the blood would be stopped by pressing the wound….. Who knows?'

I said to him like I did not remember what was the past, 'What a long story, I feel so sorry about your father. I know how it feels as I am also looking for my grandma though it is just a shattered hope. We originally planned to go to Batu Ferringhi to search for shelter but now you are saying the evacuee are going to be shifted. When??'

He replied, 'The sixth day after today... and it is going to be the last... If you miss it, that's it.' Lucas started to express his opinion like he always did, 'I guess the race with time has now started…..'

COUNTING DOWN - DAY ONE

<u>8/5/2003</u>

1 Ready to start the engine

I woke up very early this morning while the sky was still dark.

I could still see the dark sky was filled with numerous shining stars. I then saw numinous. It was so simply awesome to start the day that I would never forget. When I was still watching over the dark sky, there was never an interruption to their sleep even though the night was so freezing cold.

I spotted something unusual tonight. The boy was lying on the floor mainly because of the immobility incurred by his wound though its recovery was overall satisfactory. The rest of them were sleeping by way of sitting against the wall. I do not know if it works. It was all for the sake of security. A preparation of staying alert. The potential fight against the unwelcoming foes.

However, Kasani seemed a little bit weird tonight. I was unusually disappointed. They always seemed like twin brother and sister as if they could not be separated. It did not happen tonight. Instead, she sat on the other side of the corner where Lucas was sitting. The distance…

There must be something happening in between them. 'Is it because of what Lucas did to me yesterday?? Perhaps, she is afraid of the unforeseeable beast attack.' The invisible thing. I was asking myself. Thinking about this, I really feel frustrated as it always seems like an unresolved puzzle.

I just wanted to give up on it, but the more mysterious it seemed, the more difficult to set it all free.

Sometimes, hatred was grown as to myself regarding such personality in me. It is noxious. I was just fed up because of the repeating history. Keep thinking about this again. I just got up from my place and I went near to the window. I just took a look at the street.

It was like nothing distinctive from the street of yesterday as to the accumulating snow on the basis of that the weather yesterday was kind of fresh.

It was fairly cold to the extent that there was only the falling snowflake. It felt delightful.

I could not see any beast haunting around this area as well. It got nothing like the countable gathering last two nights ago. However, the street was bizarrely quiet. No detection of sign of lives at all. I was standing there to watch over the changes of surrounding environment from dark night to sunrise.

The sky was not cloudy today. The sun came out smoothly without any obstacles. The sunlight that slanted through the transparent glass of the gliding window. I could actually feel warm when the sun rays touched my hand. You might not know the window was not opened at all. I smiled by my own. I told myself. I got a feeling that this was going to be a good start.

2 Departure for the beginning before an end

Daniel, the boy got wounded on the left rib. I just found out his name today, when he told me to rather address him as Daniel than 'Hey, boy'. He was also confirmed to be the same age as me as well as Lucas. Daniel was kind of ready to start the race.

He told me he was okay to walk now, and apologized to me again and again for troubling me. Taking care of him made him realised what was the real meaning of 'indebted'.

I just smiled and patted his shoulder. I then said, 'Don't be silly. That's nothing to be acclaimed or complained.' After we took our breakfast at the familiar shop, we straight away walked out from the hospital like we just got discharged. I was thinking that 'How funny can things turn out to be?? As it is back to normal now, I guess.'

None of us wanted to waste our time any longer after an adequately sufficient rest. We walked in a brisk pace along the road. Surprisingly, the weather today was fairly lovely. It was pleasantly and tolerably cold.

We could walk zestfully though the depth of the snow had reached the height of our knees. The four walking kettle. Our journey had become completely weary. It was never a full stop. While we walked along Jalan Kelawai, which was by the sea side, we could actually see the large icebergs floating around the sea.

They were like many small islands found in the middle of the ocean. There were subsequently Gurney Hotel and Evergreen Laurel Hotel facing the sea.

Those aging building were looking completely intact though the only difference is that the buildings were mostly in the colour of white. The beauty of gardening right in front of the Evergreen Hotel was faded. A wasteland I saw, which got nothing but some wizened branches.

I remember how the gardener planted the decorative flowers in the garden. Cultivation they carried out. It was for manuring the plants on the land. I can only sigh about the revelation nowadays. How cruel the fact could be. Lives are merely vulnerable. Things are meant to be volatilizable due to its fugitive nature.

Despite what we saw, we continued to walk faster. So, we could find somewhere safe to stay overnight before the dark night crept in. We also hoped that we could win the race by rushing to our destination earlier before the arrival of the last ship. We almost arrived at the Gurney Plaza, which was used to be the famous shopping paradise in the multicultural island.

I was therefore reminded of the fascinating crowd in the past. Suddenly, we heard a rumble crashing boom sounded like an explosion... The Gurney Plaza fully collapsed. The walls of the building were partly imploding, but not all of them.

3 The right –sided guardian

The broken parts of the building were like falling meteors from the sky as if they were from outer space. As it required immediate reaction towards the sky falling humongous objects, it was simply unavoidable for anyone of us. However, I guess he was the exceptional one. The first thing he did was, leaning on me with his arms opened widely to hold me in. A hope for avoiding the stones or mosaic hitting on me.

I just closed my eyes tightly as I really thought all of us would just go to a place, we all called heaven. It was all in dark. I felt like I was falling asleep for a few minutes, while I kept seeing the scene on how Lucas saved me from being hit by a car.

I told myself that, 'I remember you, Lucas, the right –sided guardian.' It was all in tranquil. I tried to move but the space was too infinitesimal for me to shift my hand. I was struggling for a while that should I open my eyes or just close it.

While I was hesitating, I felt something watery dripping on my eyelashes. I was naturally responsive to the droplets. I opened my eyes undoubtedly. I saw it but I thought to be indistinguishable in the dark. It was blood!!! I recognised the smell. Lucas was right on top of me. It was his blood. He got injured!! I had to save him.

I spared no effort to get up with all my limited strength. However, I failed. I started to express my dismay by way of crying while asking Lucas to stay awake and answer me if he could hear me calling him. I was begging him repeatedly. I guess the noises I made had attracted the attention from others.

They were asking me to hold on. I just continuously woke Lucas up. They eventually moved the objects that fell down on us. It was the three of them. They survived in the name of fate. They held Lucas up, so that I could move. When I got up, I immediately turned my head towards Lucas. He was bleeding severely. The head injury was hazardous.

4 A loss in the snow

I totally went crazy as I still got many things to tell him. He could not just leave me like that. I knew he also got his little secret. I thought he had been wishing to tell for all these time. I could not lose him just like that. Based on that reason, I kept begging Mr. Samsur to save him as if he was a doctor.

I decided according to the flashback. I saw the way he performed medical treatment on Daniel. I only knew he might be able to save him. I knew he might be the capable. The tears kept streaming down my face. You are right as I did not know how to control it.

Mr. Samsur leaned to Lucas and checked his pulse. An answer of disappointment! 'I am so sorry. It was too late. He's gone.' Kasani was tearing too while she was hugging me so compactly from the back. She said, 'I feel so sorry but stay strong. You still have your grandma to meet.'

The gang just dragged me away from the cold body. Thus, by virtue of their wish, I could leave it alone in the snowy land. However, I insisted to bury him and hence, my heart would be relieved to leave. I even asked them to leave me behind. An assurance was heard. I would catch them up only after I finished completing my wish.

Having heard the voice in my heart, they decided to assist me in burying bloody body properly before we left. I stood at the place where Lucas was buried for about five minutes to mourn and apologize. I wished he would hear me. As a hope for his forgiveness of being so numb to remember who he was.

Another regret was told. I should have remembered the one who was so important to me from the start.

I watched those icy tears dropping on the roughly fluffy snow. I even heard the sound like it was squeezed affectionately. I guess it was how my broken heart sounded like. I then left together with the rest and also the thing he always brought. I think I just added one more thing to my to bring list in spite of my diary. I could really felt his existence with his belonging.

I even heard his hullabaloo at the same time when people were talking to me. I think, it was probably because of the fact only we know.

The sunset was striking us so close. The weather was getting unreasonably harsh at this time though the sun was still visible. It even dyed the sky into light purple blue. The frozen sea was being so unwelcomely peaceful. The icebergs on the ocean were literally looking like they were shifting to other places.

Their bulky body never bothered their way. It was not an illusion. Therefore, what I saw had done a logical explanation to the statement told earlier.

We just had a stop at a service station in the Tanjung Tokong area. Due to our exhausted state, we would not be able to go far. The door of the shop in the petrol station was accumulated with intensifying snow. It simply showed that the petrol station had been abandoned for quite some time.

Luckily, the door could still easily be pushed. We are just few miles closer to our destination now. I guess. I can't hold myself to ask, 'Will we make it?' This is just another mind – numbing question for me to think tonight but I feel the doubt of the undetermination as well.

The pain I learn to bear without them. I know it motivates me. I just know this could not be the end of the story. I still hope……

During this late night, my exhausted eyes are sadly opened as I am thinking about someone who makes me crying over and over again, but 'it is okay.' I am telling myself.

At least I still have my diary to accompany me. Reading back the memory I wrote about me and him, while I keep hearing Mr. Samsur murmuring about a person's name. A name which I cannot hear clearly.

DAY TWO – A SUSPICIOUS SECRECY

<u>9/5/2003</u>

1 What that girl loves

I was not in the state of deep sleep. I muzzily heard someone calling my name, 'Angela…. Angela…..' It was all in vague. I guess I was too asthenic. I felt zonked like it was a hallucination; perhaps, I was too lazy to open my eyes. I continued sleeping in spite of that person's unstoppable call. The voice was just getting incrementally louder.

I could even feel someone touching my arm. That person just put something near my hands. Due to my sense of curiosity, I decided to open my eyes forcefully. The environment surrounding me was so bright, until it did make me want to close my eyes again. My eye lids were fluttering.

I compelled myself to open my eyes gently. I saw a girl with her back facing me. She was wearing a white hood, a light yellow Baju Kurung with daisy flower prints on it. It was simply and peacefully eyed-pleasing. She was walking even further while I was calling her, 'Hi, may I know who you are?'

She just shook her head twice and then continued walking away from me. On the other hand, I wished to get up from bed to chase after her, but something from my upper body fell on the floor. I just stopped and stared at the thing on the floor for a few minute. I thought to myself, 'It was a paper goose.'

All of a sudden, I heard someone shouting, 'azLINA!! AZLINA!!' I wriggled my body shockingly and opened my eyes instantly, 'It was Mr. Samsur.' I found out. I only realised that I was dreaming just now as there was no girl wearing white cowl or even Baju Kurung here.

I looked at the floor where I sat on. There was no paper goose found either. It is a hilarious moment that I would always confuse myself with reality and dreaming. If Lucas was here, he would have waked me up by telling me to stop the non-sense. However, I knew he could never do that again even if he wished to.

Mr. Samsur was looking more anxious than I did; his cold sweat moistened his dry skin.

As I could see his peeling skin on his face and mouth like the coarse made, thick, duffel coat he was wearing now, I just thought he might not care about it. It was never his prior concern. For me and Kasani, despite our grief or any ingrained unsecured feeling, we never felt lazy to apply the travel size moisturizers as well as lip balm to avoid the gruesome consequences to happen.

2 A hidden fact

I then looked at Mr. Samsur. I did not know why, I just felt he was unusually awkward ever since the incident yesterday. After he woke up, he looked pale with his sweaty face. At the same time, I heard his jumping heart. I am pretty sure he got something concealing from us.

If I was not mistaken, I heard him calling Azlina. He never knew the name 'Azlina' sounded so familiar to me. None of us here was called Azlina. 'Who was he calling??' I asked myself. While I was thinking about the name of Azlina, Kasani went to the front door, and yelled to notify us about something.

I was like awakening from my day-dream. I gave an instant response to look towards her direction. She pointed at the fierce sky; the sky was obviously getting substantially grey. It was terrifying to think. The monstrous storm was going to start damaging this snowy wasteland all over again. I was becoming senseless at that moment.

I just ignored the question I was thinking with strenuous effort. Since Lucas had ceased to exist, Mr. Samsur had replaced the position of the team leader.

He looked unflustered and then called for a gathering of four of us. We all just discussed about this together. The way he instructed us was extraordinarily wise. His eye-sight seemed affirmatively intelligent.

He had become another person. It was totally distinctive from the one I met. The rest of them were too concentrated to notice the changes on Mr. Samsur. I was thinking that, 'What makes him look so different this time? Who is Azlina he mentioned??' I got a feeling to see whether she will be someone I previously knew.

He did not seem like he wanted to discuss with us. Instead, he commanded us to find gloves, facial masks, as well as umbrellas.

He explained to us that the winter storm would be attacking us very soon, but we could not afford to waste our precious ticking time. A risk for better now than never unless we wanted to be trapped here.

However, the wind gusts in winter storm would cause shortness of breathing. Severely, it might incur the hardly curable disease, Chronic Obstructive Pulmonary Disease. Shortness in breathing could be one of the symptoms of the said disease.

In a mild case, the patient would encounter short of breath every day. However, in a serious issue, normal activities such as walking, simple movement could become harder for the patient, because of breathlessness.

Daniel interrupted, 'Is that similar to SARS??!' That's what I heard from the people working in the centre. One of the symptoms of the said disease is difficulty in breathing??'

Mr. Samsur said, 'Nope, they are absolutely not the same, but SARS is comparatively perilous. Hence, we should use the umbrellas to assist us travelling smoothly by protecting us from the potential risk in the snow by holding the umbrellas in the same direction of the wind flow, if we walked in an opposite direction. We could do otherwise, if the wind blew in a contrasting direction.'

After the briefing, we just departed even before we took our breakfast.

He just demanded us to bring some potable snacks before we left. By reason of the visibility of the gigantic clouds, I could tell it was still very early in the morning. While we were walking like there was something going after us, the wind flow was originally mild. It was really working where we walked with the umbrellas opened as consistent as the wind flow. I realised that the dogs were not noticeable in the Tangjung Tokong area here.

3 Punishment for being rebellious??

I sincerely hoped we could actually reach the place safely. I muttered to myself with the knife I held on my right hand that, 'Lucas, I know we can do it.'

After travelling for few miles, the wind gusts started to get stronger. All I knew was that it did not seem to welcome us. We started to run fast though it did not make much difference as to walking and running in the knee length depth of snow.

We were too paranoid to the extent that we just ran with no conscious of where to go.

The rear view was getting blurry, as the wind gusts had reduced the capability of our eye-sights. The blame was on the fine snow particles whirling in the air. We tried to cover our eyes with our hands and at the same time, we kept running forward.

Finally, we found a two storey commercial centre, which seemed indestructible. So, we just went into the building without any further consideration under this exigent condition. Luckily, we were in whole.

I was panting continuously. 'Kasani, it was so close. Fortunately, we did not get lost in the winter storm. Otherwise, I don't think we would survive…..' I said with my eyes closed.

I could not get any response from her. I kept calling her name in a highly strung voice, 'Kasani…..Kasani…… Kasani……' I had eventually lost my patience. I just opened my eyes and turned my head to scan where she was, but I could not find her. I just got panic attack…. I asked the guys, 'Where is she?? Have you two seen her?? Oh, No!!'

Mr. Samsur seemed to be so steadily calm, while I was pacing back and forth like a bird with no wings. He said, 'She might have got lost until she could not follow us on the way. Don't worry, girl. I will find her. I promise.' I replied, 'I want to follow as well. I am a girl. It may be more convenient for me to help in certain circumstances.'

Mr. Samsur said, 'We have no time to waste. She is very lonely dangerous out there. If you are not afraid, you can just follow. Nevertheless, remember to obey my instruction whenever it is necessity.'

We just left Daniel alone there. We then went out. The wind gusts were so strong. I could feel my floating limbs. He asked me to hold the umbrella tightly, while searching for Kasani. I could see nothing at all along the entire search. I could only follow him. We went back to the route we were passing by.

I was tripped by something as we walked thoroughly. Mr. Samsur bent his knee down and asking me if I was okay. I replied, 'I am alright. Hey?? Is this Kasani's coat???' I ransacked the pocket of the pink jacket with snow particles sticking on it.

'Yes. Indeed. It is her. Where is she now?? Why she left her jacket here?? Her medicine is all here. I am so worried.' After I finished saying, I started crying again. I was too scared of losing another friend. 'Why people I love kept leaving me one by one?'

Mr. Samsur held me up and comforted me by saying 'It is okay. Someone might have saved her.' We went on to continue our search for one and a half hour.

It was still gainless. The weather was seriously unpleasantly cold and dry. We could only go back to the centre.

When Daniel saw us, he was in panicky and he asked, 'Have you guys found her??' I answered despondently, 'We only found her coat. I really do not know what would happen to her.'

4 I am glad you are back!!

We all just sat on the floor and said nothing at all. I really felt sour and bitter. I could not hold my tears any longer. I tried to convince myself to stay strong, but I failed. I really wished she was here. I knew I should not have invoked a rift in silence between both of us.

I missed the time when we were chatting like sisters. I missed the time we were laughing at the jotting I would make. I missed her. I was not mad at 'you'. I just did not want to get myself involved in a disastrous complication like the weather nowadays. I would never be able to do it again even if I wanted to.

Suddenly, I heard someone's footstep. I stood up in the first place and ran to the source of the noise while I kept telling myself, 'Please, Kasani… Please.. Come back to me!!'

I grinned, as my wish came true. It was her. She looked safely fatigued. I was so happy and running to her. A warm big hug in the freezing air. I guess she was too weak as she merely wore a sweater on the top to keep her warm. She later fainted and then fell on me.

Mr. Samsur and Daniel came up to me and assisted me to hold Kasani up, and then only carried her to somewhere appropriate for her to rest. I took out her medication to feed her as she had lost consciousness. After a few hours, Kasani woke up. She looked at us and the surrounding with her vacant eye-sight.

She asked with her feeble voice, 'Where am I??' I said, 'You are alright now. You are with us. I do not understand something. How did you manage to find us here??'

'It was a girl. I could not see clearly as I was giddy. She left me at the front door there. I guess it was easier for her to find me when she found me lying in the middle of snowy land.' Kasani answered.

At this moment, I noticed Mr. Samsur looked annoyingly unsecured.

I was thinking that, 'He has something to do with the girl who saved Kasani??' By the time Kasani was becoming conscious, the sky was already dark.

I went to the pathway where the located transparent front door to seek for some sufficiently bright moonlight. I started writing diary of the day. I looked up to the sky. The moon was not scarcely round.

It was not as bright as I anticipated. However, I can still see and read what I write. When I flipped back the front pages I saw the name of 'Azlina' …. 'Could it be the same "Azlina" that Mr. Samsur was murmuring about??'

AN END AT DAY THREE

10/5/2003

1 Rushing to the ending point

The sky was typically gloomy. I guess it was a trend for this time. It might also indicate that the storm was going to strike violently in latter time. I was sleeping heavily and serenely last night, unlike the previous nights. It was happening as if I already forgot about the unexpectedly dismaying tragedy.

After a well-charged night, I guess, we just walked posthaste to continue our journey. Before the beginning of the walk, I took a peep on Kasani. I still felt worried about her frail body. Although she did take her medicine to maintain the function of carrying oxygen in her body, she looked a little pale with her white lips, and her lethargic eyes made up the fretted heart. I wondered, 'Does it work perfectly?'

Despite all the disquiet concern, I still went continuing with the hope; the four of us would be able to reach the terminus for the desired reunion. I knew it was no longer safe and sound in the reputedly tranquil snowy land. The depth of the elevating snow had exceeded the height of my knee.

It truly made our travel toughly baffle. Every step I walked reminded of Lucas while it cut me an incision each time. However, the more I felt my badly infected gash, the more vigorous I had become. The wind flow started to become fairly strong. I abruptly heard a phone ringing. The ring tone sounded like an electronic composed song.

It did sound familiar to me. Despite that, I tried to ask them to see whether they were also hearing the unusual music. It was not an illusion. They also heard it. The ring tone just got louder when we walked forth. Nevertheless, Mr. Samsur demanded us not to get distracted by an unknowingly mysterious sound.

However, the ring tone just got me crazy. I really assured about the fact that this must be something related to my past. I stopped and stood there confusingly. I intended to think hard with my eyes closed compactly. It was all about the pieces of puzzle that I lost for so long. Everything was in serenity, so peacefully quiet, but later on, there was a forthcoming ice-crushing sounded like footsteps. I originally thought it was the footsteps of my companions, but when I opened my eyes, I saw a man walking towards my direction but no one else. He was a late middle-aged who had black- coloured hair, but silvery beard, wearing a nicked yellow shirt and long black pants with a thick jacket outside.

He first gave me a smirk; I suddenly passed out, and then knew nothing about the things happened next....

2 Where am I?

When I opened my eyes surprisingly, as I thought I might not be able to do this simple movement again, I still felt feeble to open them for too long. I just closed and opened my eyes repeatedly in slow motion. The surrounding was in black and white. I wondered, 'Where am I? What happened just now?'

I got a massive headache attacking me now. I thought I might just catch a cold. I felt a pain tingling on my neck for a little while. It was like I got beaten on my neck a few hours ago. The weirdest part was I did not feel as cool as the previous time. It was all peacefully warm like the bedroom I used to sleep at my house.

I later regained my strength to get up from where I was lying. I realised I was locked up in a room which had no door to be found at all whereas it seemed like a simply decorated room. There was a single bed on the right corner, a brownish wooden desk and a plastic chair. The room was painted in black colour and there was no even a window inside.

It was an overall bizarrely strange combination. I was all alone. I guess I was separated from them. They must have worried about me to the extent that they might just go searching for me all over the place. Only three days left. I wished they would not waste their precious time to find humanity. Instead, I sincerely hoped they would make it on time; perhaps, it might even be done without me.

I just thought it might be hopeless for me to get out from here to go to the evacuation centre. Due to the reason that, I did not even know when would be the existence of an exit in this mysterious room. I felt irregularly outrageous as there was electricity supply in this room though the light was too dim to see things clearly. How could he even survive without the water supply? I could still spot something on the bed. I went near to the bed. 'It is my diary book but where?? Where is the knife???'

I was searching all over the room just to find the knife. It went missing like that. I just thought, most probably it might be taken by the guy who caught me here. I really could not figure out who was that man; what was the motive he caught me here. I felt specifically thwarted about that.

I felt down and so I sat on the bed for a few hours. I then got motivated by some ingrained justification. I told myself, 'I should not give up myself just like that, as Lucas would encourage me to be otherwise.' I was thinking the logical past that 'There was a way to put me in, there must be a way out.'

I smiled and then stood up vigorously. I went circling around the room over and over again to find some sufficiently vital but trivial clues. Hopefully it could help me to get out from here.

I did spot a difference of thickness between the walls of the right side and the rest. Nonetheless, I guess I was too exhausted. I fell asleep just like that while I was still sitting on the dusty floor and with my back leaning against the 'fondly hopeful' wall. Suddenly, I felt the wall shifting, I almost lost my balance and I fell by lying on the floor.

3 An admirer???

Someone was holding me up, and asking me if I was okay. I looked up to him to see, 'It is you!! The man I saw just now?? Why you caught me here??? Do you know me?? Did I ever do something wrongful??' While asking him tans of question, I was wriggling my body to get away from him and then I moved the opposite corner there.

He left the wall opened. I could actually saw the weather outside through the transparent glass. There were books everywhere outside these four walls. The weather outside was incredibly bright. At least, I felt a little bit relieved as to the safety of my faithful companions. He came up to me and touched my left hand.

'Hi, what is your name??… It is okay.. If you don't feel……comfortable to tell…. Let.. Let me introduce myself first.' He was tongue tied. He continued to say, 'My name is Jacky…. It is your turn. Come on.' He kept blinking his eyes while he tried to fix my short messy curled hair with his left hand.

I just went backward for a few steps. It was disgustingly shocking to me. I could not hold myself to ask him, 'Why did you put me here, just let me go. We might go to the evacuation centre located at Batu Ferringhi toge~~together~~. So that, we could leave this deadly freeing island.'

He got frustrated of my attitude. He warned me by yelling me that, 'You know what?? You will never leave this place without my permission. We are not going anywhere. You will stay with me right here, right now until forever.' He just went out like that and I noticed him pushing something like a button to make the wall- like door close.

I was freaked out after hearing what he said. I was losing myself again as I did not know what was the right thing to do now. I never wanted to stay here. A strong desire. I still want to meet my grandmother. Seriously, I need to find a way out.

I heard the ring tone sound again. His hand phone could still be functionable. It was really awkward as all the electric supply and the telecommunication cable had been disabled during this time. How could it be possible for his hand phone to be used successfully??

Since then, he never opened the 'door' again for the night. It was lucky for me that I could sleep soundly for a few hours. Before I got some sleep, although the light was not meant for reading activities, I just opened up my diary.

I read to recall back the memory about someone I had lost and also recorded what had happened today. I just cannot believe that I could write my diary in this length. So that, if I die here, I hope my diary will be discovered by outsider one day to reveal this man's indecent intention!!

SHE IS MY LUCKY GOOSE

11/5/2003

1 My favourite song

I heard someone playing a song through CD player. 'Oh my pretty~~~ pretty boy~~ oh my~~~' It sounded familiar as if I heard it before. 'Where did I hear it before?? I am pretty sure it is not the first same. It is definitely not the last time.'

At this time, I felt the world was spinning. I even felt my floating footsteps when I tried to get up from where I was lying.

The room was quite reasonably large. I could see the hill right behind the backyard through the window from where I was sitting. The scenery seemed blurry but beautiful. The hill was looking hazy while the sky was still in light dark. The weather was comfortably cold.

I realised the music was sounded a little bit louder than the first few minute I heard it. Due to the call of curiosity, I went to the door of my room and opened it.

The music was being still played joyfully as I could hear someone else's singing along with the song. I walked through the corridor with the exhaustive footsteps as I did not want to attract the attention from any of them.

I was lurking in the corner of the stairway to peep over the situation down the stairs. I saw a girl. She was singing and dancing in front of the table where the CD player was placed on. She was approximately at my height and she was wearing the white cowl on her head and a Baju Kurung which had daisy flower prints on it.

She had reasonably fair skin which was in contrast with the colour of the Baju Kurung she was wearing. While I was still standing up the stairs, she looked to my direction, 'Come down here and join me, my darling.' I walked out from the corner, and I then smiled, 'Hi, do you know me?'

'Of course, I do. Don't you remember??' She said. Her friendly looking smile made me wanted to come closer. I went down the stair laboriously, while the music was still played repeatedly. I saw her holding something in her right palm but I could not see unintelligibly. I stopped to walk further at a few steps away from her.

She walked slowly to me. She opened up her small palm and showed me what was she holding for all these while. When the riddle was resolved, I saw a paper goose. 'Now you know.' She said.

I closed my eyes and opened again by entailing a great effort. I only realised it was merely a dream. I was still in the room with no door found at all on the face of my sight.

2 He is a disguised demon

The hanged bulb on the wall was oscillating. I was staring at the swinging bulb and I was only awakened after I heard the ring tone of the guy's phone.

I guess it was ringing again. 'This was exactly the song I heard in my dream but its only difference was that one of them was sounding like a self- tuned music, and on the other hand, the other one was rhythm and blue. It was a kind of popular music in the 1940's particularly from blue music. However, its accompany with electrically amplified instruments made it sound young.

It was amazingly unjustifiable. How could the phone be used while the cable was not working?? How could even the bulb here lighting while there was no electric supply?? Did he have his own reserved supply?? But how long the supply would last?? Despite those entire mind – storming questions, the wall opened again.

He came in and asked me to take my stuffs. He then pulled me up from the bed and brought me out of the room. I struggled. I tried to get his hand off me, 'Hey, where you are taking me?? Get your hand off me!!!' He was like a brazen alien, as ignorance was the thing he ever knew and he just kept dragging me out of the room. I knew this would never be the truth.

He thrust me to a chair and then tied me up with synthetic rope. He took a box of make up set and applied on the dull face. I really got annoyed, 'Stop!! What you are doing!!???' After his make up session which he thought he was skilful at, he untied me and brought to a mirror.

I was almost fainted when I looked myself in the mirror. I looked extraordinarily white with the foundation he applied on my face while my cheeks were outstandingly red. He never tried to tidy my messy hair but he used his old red ribbon hair clip on it. I looked abnormally insane.

He then brought me to the front of a cupboard. He took a dress out from it and leaned the dress to me to see whether it fitted me or not. The dress was in striking bloodily red colour. I was terrifically shocked. White face, red ribbon and red dress. I strongly resisted to wear it.

He forcefully wore the dress on me just like that. I looked tubby after wearing the dress as I was still having my thick jacket on. I looked extremely hilarious.

This did not seem perilous but it was totally unacceptable. What was wrong with him? What was he doing? He was then impelling me to the front door of the bookstore. He held my arm so tightly as if I would run away.

The diary I kept in my jacket, had made my body felt tingling, due to the tightness of the dress on the outer layer. I was so scared I would drop it, so I just used my the other hand to hold it tight in order to prevent the undesirable consequence. He got me out of the door and I was thrown in the snow.

3 It is her!

He then took out the rope again and tried to tie me up. I was squirming in the snow. The snow was really cold. I could feel my hand become numb. I was screaming emphatically. Hopefully, someone would hear my scream as to seeking for help and coming over to save me. He laughed reprehensibly, 'You can scream as loud as you can as no one will hear you in this wasteland. Let me light you up with fiery fire to burn you out.'

He tied me up so tight and took out a green coloured mini lighter. I was frightened but I could only scream and yell with my eyes all closed as my mobility was restricted. I just thought that this might be the tragic ending for me to take my very last breath at this time. I heard a horrible shriek. I opened my eyes shockingly.

He was lying on the fluffy snowy ground. A girl was standing right behind where he was lying down. I was confusingly wondered. She looked so familiar, like the girl I saw last night in my dream though she was wearing a different dress code.

She was putting on long cotton made trousers and a pink coloured sweater on the top while a white duffel coat she wore as an outer jacket. The specialty was about her white hair scarf with a daisy hair pin on the scarf.

She came closer to me and said, 'Angela, don't worry. I will untie you.' I was too catastrophically scared to speak anything.

She saw my uncomfortable expression, whereby she said, 'It is ok. It is me. Azlina. Don't feel scared. The bad guy passed out because of my incredibly delicate strike with only my bony hand attacking his neck. Remember me?? I am your lucky goose.' She held me up as I felt lull on my unwilling immobility.

She said, 'Let leave this place before he wakes up.' I said, 'But before we leave, I need to find something.' She took out the knife and asked, 'Is this the one you are looking for??'

I grinned, 'Thank you. Azlina.' Suddenly I was awakened by the name of 'Azlina'. She is the one who appeared in my diary. The one I have not seen for years. I could not hold myself anymore. I gave her a big, heart warming hug, and she did too.

After we left the bookstore safely, I just asked her to clarify my doubts. 'How do you know that I was caught there??' 'I tailed you at the back ever since I saw you at the area in the vicinity of the grocery…..' She just stopped continuing here.

'So, you were the one!!! Why you wanted to tail me while you could have just came out and greet. By the way, where have you been for all these while?? I was looking for you but it was a mere failure of attempts.' I kept asking continuously.

'If I came out earlier you would have been killed by the weird guy, am I right?... I also didn't want to get disappeared. My father … he ….' Her sorrow crept in and she did not seem to be capable to continue. Her beautiful gleaming eyes were telling something elegiac. Therefore, I also kept quiet to reduce the anxiety between us.

We tried to travel speedily to get to the evacuation centre despite I was mentally too groggy to walk after a torturing night. I did ask her about grandma to see whether there was any fortunate coincidence but the answer was still despondent.

However, I will still keep my hope alive. The motivation I need for all of us to keep on going as I never wanted to give up.

We only got into a card game shop to stay overnight. I told her about the news of untimely death of Lucas and also the story that I had been going through. She did not look much surprise as what I initially contemplated.

The outrageous part is that she never mentioned to me about the period where she went missing. However, by observing her micro-expression as well as facial demeanour, I could tell it must be something catastrophic. It was unpleasant moment to tell.

There must be something more she intends to hide. I did not ask her further. This is the way I trust our friendship.

After lending her handkerchief for me to wipe out the make up of my face, she falls asleep in the very early night. By looking at the red dress I wore in the morning, I only realise my stomach is vociferating in the abandoned site.

It is all empty here but a roof to shroud. I guess the hungry stomach is just groaning, which cause me to lose my sleep tonight. I went to sit at the front door again under the bright, coldly warming moonlight with this diary in my hand.

THE FATHER AND THE DAUGHTER

<u>12/5/2003</u>

1 Going through the time tunnel

I was in the state of magnanimous sleep. I slept to forget to wake up in the morning today.

The light from the transparent glass of the front door slanted into the house, specifically where I was lying right beside a book shelf. The books I made use by making them as my paper pillow which my head was lying on.

It was an overall good night sleep. I would not want to wake up by keep flipping my eyelids. The sun had come out. Its light was extraordinarily dazzling. I could barely see Azlina. She was standing right in front of the front door though the image reflected in my eyeballs was not really unambiguous.

However, I just knew it was her. Her white hair scarf on her head as well as the daisy hair clip. I just thought back about the old days during the time when she came to my house to stay for few nights. It was because of my durable persistence in inviting her to come. The way she was welcomed.

She originally rejected my offer due to the fact that she felt bashful. She always thought that she only wanted to save it for trouble. Moreover, I only met her again after a long separation.

So, I kept asking the same question by exaggerating the fact but I, indeed, needed a personal home tutor. Failure in the next coming exam was the nightmare of mine in the past.

It was a minor fib. She doesn't know my real intention until now. My irresistible invitation. I now thought back about my naivety insistence. The nights we spent together. I laughed by my own when I thought of the happy hour both of us went through.

How we were chatting in the middle of the night while we needed to wake up early to school. As a result, how we got punished by standing outside the class for half an hour.

It was a piece of mine. I think she should know I never wanted to forget. This was really sweet and sour. It was hilariously nostalgic memorable picture to me. Amazingly, I did not feel as much hungry as I felt yesterday in this morning. I thought 'Was it because of going through the time tunnel?'

It had made me fell into the state of timeless. I wondered, 'Is it because I was not really existed at this moment? Perhaps, I did not realise my existence at this time??'

When Azlina noticed a sweetly eerie smile, she came to me and asked what made my day. A denial was appreciated on what I felt and said, 'No, nothing. I was just feeling hungry. I do feel a little bit worried as I do not have any confidence. Whether we will reach the final destination on time.'

She replied, 'Why do you worry about unpredictable things? Tomorrow is just another mystery. Come on, let's go out and start our adventure since you said you are hungry.'

2 What a coincidence!!

We walked out from the store to hunt for foods like what the beasts do. The weather was unreasonably warmer today though the friendly atmosphere seemed cloudy.

According to previous horrendous experience as to winter snow, we both were unconfident to agree to our weather forecast. How it could be a funnily unscathed day. I guess??

We walked with faintness as we were running out of energy without any replenishing. We were getting slow down on each step we were taking. We still hanged on. It was a quite peaceful street today as I heard serenity. The depth of snow was remained the same. This was also the reason why we felt worn out.

We continued walking until we saw a mini hypermarket. We stopped for gasping of lungful air. We thereby could restore the strength used. We walked to the store, tried to open the gate. Surprisingly, it was like we were welcomed to go into this brand new stop. Someone had left the store opened on purpose.

The store was quite dark on the ground that the gate was not composed of transparent glass.

The reasonably glaring sunlight just could not slant through but I could feel the wind flow whispering at the back of my ears. The murmur sounded dangerous.

Based on that gut feeling, a quest to stay focus. The rigorously attention was contributed on what we saw, whereas I got my shaky hand ready on the defensive weapon. So, I would provide an immediate response to the uncongenial foes.

We walked slowly in the fairly cold air. We did fumble for unknown objects as we could not see properly what was in front of us. Azlina inadvertently stumbled and leaned to a shelf, I tried to hold her from falling. However, I fell on her instead. We were screaming obstreperously while the stuffs arranged from the shelf kept falling like feather meteors.

They were just packets of instant noodle. It was too lucky for us. I was scared of those faithful eyes would be shut permanently. I thought I saw torchlight on the shadowy floor. I fumbled to reach it in the dark. Finally, I got it and just turned it on. I illuminated around. I saw all the groceries dispersed all over the place.

There was nothing hazardous to be found. While we were picking up some foods, I heard someone talking from far. It sounded clamorous. 'We still cannot find her!! Where could she possibly go??.... We should just move on!!'

It was all in welter. The voice sounded familiar to me, I stood up and flashed the light to the source, as we walked closer. 'Who's that?' I saw them!!!!

It was Kasani and the rest of them. They were still here. Guiltiness was felt. It was unexpected. An indirect cause to encumber them to be caught here. I came up to them, 'Kasani, Mr. Samsur, and Daniel. It's me, Angela.' I told them about my very heart-thrilling odyssey. They looked stunning. I guess belief was too hard to gain by this funnily insane adventure.

Kasani told me, 'You were lucky!!' I explained, 'It was just because of my paper goose. Come, Azlina ...' A voice from the back with avidity, 'Azlina!!' The shadow in the dark came closer, 'Father??'

3 He is the culprit!

Azlina ran to Mr. Samsur, 'Father??' Mr. Samsur said, 'It's really you!!! I thought you were dead!!!....' He felt uncannily ill at ease to continue. Azlina took a deep breath repeatedly and groaned. The complication was still unrevealing.

Daniel became the first to be impatient and said, 'It is not the time to chit chat now. Since we have found Angela, let's go. You two can do chit chatting on the way.'

We just continued our journey. The harbor is still far away. The night was getting closer. We just stopped at a music store. It was a quiet night. Everybody was sleeping quite early except for the big head. I just shut my eyes without sleeping. I guess I was not the only one. I could hear Azlina talking to her father in the corner.

Mr. Samsur said, 'Fortunately, you survived. I really don't want to lose you like how I lost your mother.'

Azlina replied delicately but in angst tone, 'If you really cared about both of us, you would not be disappearing for ten years. You now came back to redress the mistake. It is unscrupulously precarious, father. Do you know how many lives we, Malaysian had lost because of your self-indulged passionate towards winter science.. I don't even understand how it was formed in the first place.'

'I knew it was my fault to cause all these undesirable troubles. I did try to fix it but the fate seemed to go against it. I swore to you. When I brought you to my experimental lab, I just wanted to show you. The successful creation of a dab of snowflakes. I really did not know. A split of water because of your madness towards me and then the explosion to the snow converting machine I created..'

'Are you trying to tell me it is my fault?' Azlina's face changed moodily.

'I never knew the explosion of the used laser machine would create the skirmish of two air masses of substantial gap in between temperatures and moisture levels.. That's what I tried to understand. When the two air masses mingled, in other words, it would be addressed as a front. If cold air advanced and pushed away the warm air, it formed a cold front. Therefore, it led the warm air advanced, it would rise up over the denser. The cold air mass and therefore the formation of a warm front. As a consequence, it reduced the temperature here. How it provokes a life-taking winter storm.'

I stood up and said, 'What!! You, the evil conductor behind all the mess.......' I guess my perturbed voice had woke others up.

Daniel said, 'What's wrong?? We need to rest here. So that, we would get to the centre on time. Tomorrow is the last day ...' Azlina quickly came up to me. She requested to cease the talking. She then asked everyone to continue sleeping.

Mr. Samsur turned his head away when I laid my eyes on his face. I thought, 'Is it a guilty demeanour Azlina said to me politely?' 'Please, Angela. Keep it down. I know for sure that you also don't want to make things worse. There is no time for executing the blame. We only have one more day expiring or perhaps that's it. We have to give corporation to make things work.'

I stunned for awhile. I just could not believe this. I also did not know how to deal with it. I just kept quiet and laid down on the place where I did previously.

The latter night seemed more quiescent. On the other hand, there was a silently violent wave attacking my heart. I was turning over again and again along the night while other people were sleeping smoothly.

I went out and sat on the icy pavement outside the store. The moonlight is just like a giant lighting bulb. I hereby start writing my diary in the tranquil night.

At the same time, I wonder, 'Will the answer be written on the moon? Could she tell me how far she is at right now?'

THE LAST SHOT

13/5/2003

1 Unbearable discombobulation

I dreamt about grandma last night. She was trapped in a snowy landslide at our house. She yelled for help pathetically but no one could hear or reach her out. She was drearily lonely in the dark. She could not even move her limbs.

She later called my name feebly. I tried to go near, but she was getting farther. She was literally shifted backward. It was awkward.

She eventually disappeared in my dream. I then woke up with my mouth widely opened because of the suffocation. The loss of the opportunity to see the outstanding face again. As she could only exist in my dream now. I was thinking that if all these incidents never happened.

Wouldn't it be the perfect days? I would most probably be together with my grandmother right now, and Lucas would not have died in the dismaying way.

It is so cruel in the sense that we have to watch the people to die in freeze. Some of their bodies are not even found, though the land is free from the virulent affection of SARS. There might be any living organism to survive and no exception for the SARS viruses.

It is a deadly regret. I don't intend to blame him, but he made it happened in the way that no one could turn it over.

I wished I could. Everything was going back to the way it used to be. By thinking about how I perceived him to be a nice guy, and an intelligent one. However, it was all ruined.

An arrangement or not. That conversation about the accidental ravaging passionate to our motherland. I just could not start a greeting even if I wanted to. It was all as cold as the weather.

I guess I just laid my hatred to him instead, whenever I was reminded of my loss. I knew I had made a bestowal to Azlina. Save it for moving on instead of creating trouble.

I remember the words of working together with a consistent effort in order to achieve the united goal. However, I was struggling heavily.

I was afraid that I could not hold myself any longer. Therefore, a decision of being soundless..

While we were walking together, a purported alienation from the solely majority crowd in the middle of besnowed island. This was the thing I could ever do best at this moment.

According to the obliged blame taker, the evacuation centre should be right at the end of the downhill street. It is opposite the roundabout where the Queen Victoria Memorial Clock Tower is located. There were still a few kilometres away from where we were. A minuscule eagerness and enthusiasm was felt like it was too easy to forget the saturnine detestation.

2 Got you!!

We did not really consume much nourishing sustenance in the morning. It was because of we knew the fact. It was undoubtful as we were running out of time. We were evolutional to rush like a speedy car on the race track. The junk foods in our pockets were meant to be used in a greater necessity even though the call of the hungry mouths.

The sky was still like it was a crisp with unfavourable temperature. Although I woke up early this morning for our prepared departure, I felt the skin on lip was scantily ripping. The severity should not deserve an ignorance. Prevention is always better than cure. I consistently applied what my lips needed to be replenished about.

The depth of snow here was not really fathomless as it only reached my calf. It did make the wayfare become smoothly while alleviating the fatigued state of mind. The sun was not as dazzling as how it was like yesterday.

All of a sudden, the wind became unexpectedly strong as contrast as how we envisaged. We almost tumbled. I dropped my diary. The memorable knife was found on the floor simultaneously. I squatted down to pick up. These are the two pertinent things in my whole life. No tolerance of the risk of loss. The snow then started falling on my body profoundly with lacking of intensity of weight.

I looked up to the sky. It turned aggressively grey. It seemed like the freezing rainstorm going to hit at any time. The snow man was commanding again to walk laboriously quicker to find somewhere to hide. He warned us, 'We would never want to know what would be incurred next during the winter storm.

We just followed what he requested in spite of my unwilling obedience. I know well about my rebellious trait. After a few minute of walking, I heard a bellow of rage fusing with the noise made by the wind gusts. I was not hallucinating as four of them also heard it.

At this moment, I forgot to breathe. My limbs were shivering as in the first time I heard this roaring howl. I tried to calm down and resumed to breathe. Mr. Samsur asked us to run in the opposite direction from the source of the noise. So, we ran forward.

Unluckily, while we were running arduously, a vigorous howl was heard from far at the direction we were heading.

We thought it might not be a dead end to go on the right, and therefore we ran to the right. We then heard the same monstrous calling at that direction. The snow man with his invincible determination. The heart of survival did not want to give up. He guided us to go to the left.

Despite our strenuous attempts for escaping, failure was waiting as we were encircled by unidentified 'beasts'. The preying game they were playing with our debilitated minds. As the wind was raging wildly until we lost the visibility to the environment around us.

I put my diary in an appropriate place. The prevention in the deadly fight. I took the knife and got those shaky limbs ready to provide immediate responses. We all were standing back to back in a circle with our heads looking over all the directions. The noises started to dispel for a few minutes.

3 The white flag we could never have a chance to raise

I abruptly heard Kasani screaming in a bleak and desolate tone. I turned my head around. It was the dogs. They attacked Kasani. It was too vigorous to see. I heard some noises from my way. I just turned my head back. I quickly responded by taking out the knife and brandishing the knife randomly.

I did manage one of them but the rest kept hunting me down violently. I was bitten by their razor-edged like teeth to the extent that they could still bite through and tear out my thick jacket and sweater. I was then dragged away from where I originally stood.

I was hurt severely. The wound on me looked murky. I did not even want to look at it because it was disgustingly startling. I did not let go of my solely offensive weapon to protect myself from getting digested gastronomically. I knew Lucas was still with me in this fight.

As I never wanted to be ending my life in this way, I took a long breath and clung on the courage in the fate of death. I aimed accurately. Acts of merciless were shown like how Lucas did previously. It was not intended so I had to apologize.

After ending the fight with the beasts, I pressed hard on the wound of my right hand. I walked forward to find the rest of them.

However, all I saw was a pool of blood absorbed by the snow. It made the snowy land looked scarily and ominously reddish. I felt wobbly as my head tended to fall. I tried to look up but the world was spinning. It was unstoppable.

I just walked continuously with the casualty I was holding closely. I just got to act quick. My blood was dripping swiftly even when I tried to stop bleeding. Pressing hardly on the wound was never a good idea.

4 A last good bye

I then saw a small wooden cottage. I went in to get a rest as my eyes were forcefully opened. Nevertheless, I still took a rigorous check on the surrounding to evade the saddening attack. I used my ripped jacket to wrap up the wound and then a notice of the companied wounds. They were found on my back and my lab as well.

A whisper of intuitive feeling showed the end of the story. I was caught with idealess mind. I just kept gasping for air. I took out my diary and then started writing the ending of this disenchanted wayfare. We still could not get out of this isolated island.

There are tans of flashback about the memory of my childhood especially right before my parents died. The lovely darling smile on my gratifying grandmother.

The selfless sacrifice just to allow me to live for second time, but unfortunately, I disappointed him. At this moment, I felt thirsty. I was reminded of the previous scene to hold back from the hunger of fresh blood. I thought I could be turning into something horrible soon like what happened to him previously. However, I hope to overcome the thirst as I was not born with it.

My body is shivering……

Despite the discomfort urge, Lucas had been appearing in my drunken mind. I had been going back too much lately. It never seemed to stop. I wished to be granted a chance to say sorry if we could ever meet in heaven.

The bloody goose on my slow moving hand. I think of the very first friend I made bizarrely. Kasani, the girl who reminded me of the promise made……

I just could not believe how unforeseen death had been so near. It was all pathetic and miserable even from the beginning of our life. I really wish the explosion of the snow converting machine never existed in the first place, so that all these spells would be broken. Although we might still be under the ghastly affection of SARS viruses…..

Nonetheless, I am now getting sleepy sluggardly….

GENUINELY UNAUTHENTIC

4/12/2014

1 Struggling in bewilderment

Today was the first day I got back home after staying at the hospital for so long. I felt like entering a stranger's house.

By looking at the surrounding, it seemed like the old days. I could still see the old CD player right on the desk near the stairway. Although it did look a little outmoded, it was still functionable. I walked up the stair to my room. It was right opposite of the staircase. Lucky me! A second chance to walk through this door.

The design of my room reminded me of what I had. The white window pane is as consistent with the wall. There is my dark brown wooden antique clock on the wall. It was located right opposite my single sized bed. I could still remember that I was the one who placed it there.

The reason why?? I could still remember that I was always late for school. Grandma advertently made it as a special timer. As it would be thirty minutes faster.

Therefore, I would have a misperception. It was a brilliant idea though I would still be slacking. However, it was a history breaking record to tidy up myself before I departed to school.

It is still a very funny moment. I spotted something on my desk. I went near to have a closer look. It was my diary book contained in the wooden box. My clean hands remained by touching it. It seemed to have a carved picture of footprints on it. I took out the diary book and flipped through the book.

I thought there was something I wrote before I got into coma, which was equally worse as the vegetative state. Originally, when I first woke up, I could not even know how to speak and move. Furthermore, my ability to think was slow to the extent that the remembering capacity was pathetically and awfully degenerating.

I could not even remember my name at that time. Nevertheless, I remembered the part as to snowing in Malaysia in pieces. I kept dreaming about it, but I did not know how to tell. I looked out the window at the hospital where this familiar scenery was playing in my mind over and over again.

The land outside the park was not snowy and everybody was wearing normal shirt; instead of the thick, duffel coat that we would only wear in winter.

It was so distinctive from what I had seen formerly. I thought, 'Is it back to normal??' My principal doctor, which was Doctor Fazlim. The young man I used to see, had become a middle-aged man. Anyway, he still charmed the amazed eyes. He was solely in-charged of prescribing and applying medication on me.

After I went through a few lessons of physiotherapy, I started to get back on track. The crook handle walking stick helped me a lot like how grandma used it. Speaking about grandma, I was really flushed with exultation to see grandma again. The first sight on her wrinkled face, I burst into tears as a result of the untold feeling. An apology is still owed as I should have said to her in the earlier time.

2 Gentle heart to care

She patiently taught me to speak ever since I woke up from my so called hibernation. She even brought me a mini recorder, where it contained all of my favourite songs, namely 'Pretty Boy'. She would always play the song once a week during the time of the sealed sight.

She had all sorts of music to be played revolving my ears; I would thereby be able to catch up the language. She knew all the hopes.

The two months time in the hospital before I could actually be discharged from the hospital. In order to improve the function of the hibernated brain, the reason why the guitar was there.

It was as fascinating as I was used to feel when I saw it. Nevertheless, only limited rhythms were played with the familiar cords.

The rhythms were all in pieces. 'It did sound complete.' That's the small lie she told. I don't know why, the fondly pleasant day I would always have when I was with the guitar.

It improved as time passed by. Based on my scattering pieces of memory, I found the song that Lucas had written, 'The lucky star'. A quick action to write before it disappeared in the depth of memory. It was bashful to say that it was my simple composition of the song. It was unbelievably staggering that I could play the long lost song.

Amazingly, I found something in the drawer of the desk in my ward. There were many of them. The beautiful wishes in the birthday cards I had been receiving throughout the years as an observation told that the cards did seem yellowish. I took out and read.

The first card I read was from Rehan. Those words crumbled my weakest part. 'Happy Birthday, Angela. We are waiting for you to come back to school, so that we might be entering the singing competition together. I was used to dislike singing as you know my shyness. However, I will do it for you, so please wake up..' It was dated 04/12/2003.

Most of them were dated 04/12/2003. There was one. The name of 'Kasani' was seen on a hand-made birthday card.

'Hello, Angela. I am Kasani. I am the one who stays at five rooms away from your room. Nice to meet you though you might not hear me. Your grandmother has been such a nice person. She would invite me to enjoy her delicious homemade cuisine for almost everyone in the same floor as you stay. She hopes that you would actually feel bored to be a sleeping beauty one day.'

At this time, a literal confusion about the memory I had inside my brain. 'Wasn't she dead at that time, was she?? How could it possible she could still write birthday card for me??' I started to make myself talking. A question was posted to grandma about this girl. It was for the hope of seeing her again. Grandma replied, 'She was the girl who used to live here for two years and was struggling with the anemia disease.'

However, she got fully recovered after the successful operation in regard to the removal of her spleen. In other words, a ductless vascular gland, located in the left upper abdomen near the stomach. It was because they found in latter time that the red blood cells were severely damaged at a bizarrely high rate. After she left, no one here has ever not seen her again.

3 The dead came back to live

I was caught in the state of chaos after hearing the past in the familiar space. The mess was like all in the aftermath of the tornado disaster. No knowledge on how to differentiate what was real in my memory.

I never told grandma about this insensibility. She is surely not capable for the age of anxiety anymore. Someone else was more suitable. I said, 'Doctor Fazlim, can I ask you a question?' He replied gently, 'Yes, of course.'

I tried to be frank. I therefore asked with no further hesitation, 'Can you still recall the year of 2003?? The ice age??' He looked exaggeratedly shocking, 'Besnowing?? In Malaysia??' He then started laughing, 'What incident supporting your imagination? I never seen the phenomena of snowing in Malaysia.'

I said, 'Really?? But why I would have memories about snowing in Malaysia if I never gone through it? Furthermore, the people existed in my dream, are genuine in reality.'

Pride was swallowed. 'For example, we met in my dream, as my principal doctor, Doctor Fazlim. Isn't it weird??' I got horrified for awhile. As I thought I might invade the wrong space at the wrong time or I might have travelled to the other side of the world in the saintly secret place.

Doctor Fazlim could not hold the laugh back. He tried to illustrate explicitly and calmly, 'Don't you worry, I guess any external stimulation would possibly be received during the years you were in coma. Your enabled brain might translate or transform the external factors into your very own personal messages in your brain.'

It did seem like you were communicating with or updating yourself about any upcoming environment indirectly in the unique method though no conscious at all. I was told to imagine that the dream you had during your long night sleep.

It was quite normal for the patient like you. In the sense that the electrical charges derived in nerve impulses transmissions in your brain was still passively active, though the severe head injury.

Although I have survived after the brain operation of blood clot removal...

He told, 'Do you know that you never woke up from the day you got hit by an illegal lorry driver? The driver was still a teenage boy when he drove the lorry. He got caught after the day you were admitted to hospital.'

By having this in mind, I quickly flipped back the diary to where I had stopped writing. I was with my empty shell momentarily. I was staring at the mirror on the desk as I could not believe what I saw. The blank pages after the paper dated 04/12/2002. It was the last page of the diary on that date.

The snowing experiencing was merely a dream. It was all made up by incorporating the revelations I got to know in reality. The mixture of the absurdity in the imagination with the truth. A comparison of the dates. It was twelve years gap. It was hard to believe that time passed like I am not the naive teenager girl anymore.

4 The lie time told

It was cruel. How the time I had during my adolescence was vanished. I lost it in a long sleep until the gaps in memory were filled with illusion. I guess I could never get it back unless the presence of the time machine, but I was pretty aware of the fact of possibility.

A birthday celebration party was held today. She thought I should celebrate my birthday mightily. The big day as to recovery improvement whereby I was discharged from the hospital.

I knew I should be at downstairs soon after hearing noises coming from the living room. I put on the new white sweater and the red knee length skirt. Talking about this brand new outfit, it fitted my body perfectly. I should have felt glad. She said it was finally done. The first dress ever she bought me this year.

I could tell tears were trembling in the whitish blue wrinkled eyes. I could tell her regret in the white soul. She must be brought back to old times frequently. She might think if things happened differently, there might be no trigger of unforeseeable consequences. I should be blamed instead for the highly sensitive nature.

By preparing my birthday party, she has been happily exhausted. To devoid her walking up the stairs, so I came down from the stair swiftly.

I saw my classmates in primary school and my gang. They all just came up to me. The numerous heart-warming hugs were all at the same time. I was totally melted like the ice-cream cone under the hot sun. It was too gay to meet the long lost friends even though something was missing.

The engaged catering service was cool. Compliments were received as our very own Malaysian cuisine. I guess things has not been the same in the present time. I knew she dreamt about this for a long… long time.

This was something she lives to see. Everybody in this party was mingling. Although there were soft conversations, loud noises were heard from the compact crowd.

5 The crowd I was used to know?

I saw him, the class monitor. Michael, the one I remember the most in my class, was also here. He came up to me and greet by way of shaking my right bony hand. He was not wearing the round framed glasses I loved anymore.

He really became mature though there was nothing changed. A technical behaviour was shown to be a grown adult unlike me. He said, 'I am punished for leaving my girl behind because of my celebration party.'

At this time, I wondered that who would be the lucky girl. If she was someone I knew, he would have brought her here. I felt a little frightened to see what would I see next. I was asked to provide so called mobile phone numbers. He even took out his multifunctional phone to take pictures in order to upload it to the social network. The advance technology I missed.

This is something I never foresaw. I was surprised enough to find out how mobile phone could be this small and thin like a notebook I would always bring to school last time.

I did not own anything like this before in my whole life but I did see people using it. For example, my grandma's phone. I mean the one used to be her phone.

It was reasonably huge but thick. It could only be used to make calls or text messages.

The function changes nowadays. People use their phones in many aspects; such as notebook, phone book, photo album, alarm clock, or even an information centre through Google.

I am truly amazed by what I never perceived. I do understand that the world is evolving rapidly. As I already missed in these time, that's what the conclusion permanently is.

I was conversing with my gang in secondary school. Esther told me that she had finally become an official executor for justice whereas Rehan had just been the wife of other last year. Regarding Joyce, the girl with naivety, still wants to enjoy life with unlimited freedom. Their retinas brought me to the fact. How time flied at this moment like I wished I could be paralysed by it again.

Someone was knocking the front gate. I strangely subdued as I stood up from the sofa and looked out. The ambiance outside was quite dark due to the dim street light.

I could not really see who were standing outside. When I walked nearly to the front gate, I saw Lucas. I was very happily blossomed right before I saw Azlina holding his right arm.

6 The chance I lost!

I suddenly smiled unnaturally with my head looking to other direction. Lucas said, 'Hi, Angela. Long time no see. It is really a pleasure to see you again.'

Azlina consequently said by mimicking Lucas's word, 'Hi, Angela. How are you? Have not seen you for so long... You still look like the one in the past. I wish you happy birthday and also want to congratulate you that you just gave up in being a sleeping beauty. We straight away came back from Sarawak when I heard it from my brother about the rousing good news.'

I knew from how they behaved as well as the rings they wore on their ring fingers. I could not even feel disappointment. It was like something I previously knew. Although I knew it was hopeless to ask this question, I did it anyway. I said, 'Congratulation to you two too.'

Azlina replied, 'Oo, you mean the wedding rings. Thank you my dear.' She then hugged me while my eyes were caught by Lucas's uncomfortably anxious eye-sight, he later looked away from me. A guessing was made. He just would not want to be reminded of our past.

Despite the awkward moment, I still invited them to come in while Azlina passed a paper bag from her hand to me. She told me that she was not really disappearing twelve years back. She just went together with her adoptive mother except for his brother.

They were back to her father's hometown in Sarawak. It was sadly for taking care of him soon after she got an official phone call from the local authority. Her father was suffering from one kind of mental disease, called Hallucinogen Persisting Perception Disorder (HPPD).

I bet you never knew about this disorder where it had been categorized as continual presence of sensory disturbance.

'I did come back. My brother did not go back to our house as he had been living in the provided accommodation. Therefore, I only noticed the stack of letters in my letter box. I only then found out about your grandma… I just went to Lucas's house for discussing on how to settle this fall out…. I am sorry.. Angela.'

She stopped talking with her head looking down the floor. The sorrow in words. I tried to make things right by comforting her that 'It's alright. Darling. Now I have cleared the doubt that has been haunting me for so long. I should say thank you instead. Thank you.'

I looked at her. The grief swimming in my head and the tears were like sharp blades that slit a deep and narrow cut in my heart though all the best wishes were sincere for this newly married couple..

7 Pretence makes up suffocation!

After the end of the party, I went back to my room and hid under the blanket on my bed. I was trying to express the dismay in me in silence. Grandma should not be burdened by reason of the twisted fate. I am lost in defining true love.

However, I knew she should not behave in this way. I should feel satisfied of the second chance I was given. I oblige to appreciate what I have right now in the name of serenity of this wonderful land.

The very least, those depressed eyes are still able to observe lives. I look out of the window. The moonlight is gleaming in the sky like telling me that the stage is her. It is not a windy night today.

I can hear dogs communicating by barking at each other. The street lights is not as bright as the moonlight. Nonetheless, I still see the pedestrians who wear plain T-shirt and short pants. They were walking on the pavement with a few paper bags on their hands.

It is still the same weather, but not any winter storm that could kill hundred thousand of people at one time. I really feel glad that Malaysia is still the conventional Malaysia. The land is full of vitality with different graceful cultural element. I just love the way Malaysia originally is. I will never want to change my beloved land. I guess this is just the way I show my love to you.

I know time will heal. The rain in this summer time will stop somehow in future. All I need is time to let go of someone I used to feel so close. The love's beyond infinity.

To him, it was long gone but I am still thinking about what if in my head. The sound of my broken heart is murmuring in my mind. So, can only write it down before I could get a sleep in a tranquil night.

Dancing in the rain
You are my favourite songs
I have been singing all day long
Try not to play the music in my mind.
I know you can't

Sorrow plays the role
When she became the one to stay
Try not to remember what I have lost
I know you can't.

All I want to do is
Dancing in the rain
Dancing in the rain
Playing my favourite songs
Dancing in the pouring rain

She is my paper goose
I even held on with my eyes closed
It is still white in colour
You know I will
Your smile in my heart
Still melts to sweep away the pain
It is still at the place
You know it will

All I want to do is
Dancing in the rain
Dancing in the rain
Playing my favourite song

Dancing in the pouring rain

It's just like phantom
Follow me everywhere
No one sees it but you
You know nothing changes~~~
So, just

Dancing in the rain..
Dancing in the rain ….rain~~~
Playing my favourite songs .. songs~~~
Dancing in the pouring rain … Oh.. Oh…
Good night, all time summer land!

(THE END)

Printed in the United States
By Bookmasters